The
Cape Cod
Caper

Other Penny Spring and Sir Toby Glendower Mysteries

MARGOT ARNOLD

The Cape Cod Caper

A Penny Spring and Sir Toby Glendower Mystery

A Foul Play Press Book

The Countryman Press
Woodstock, Vermont

TO JANE, FOR THE CRANBERRY BOG
&
THE 12 O'CLOCK SCHOLARS

WHO'S WHO

GLENDOWER, TOBIAS MERLIN, archaeologist, F.B.A., F.S.A., K.B.E.; b. Swansea, Wales, Dec. 27, 1926; s. Thomas Owen and Myfanwy (Williams) G.; ed. Winchester Coll.; Magdalen Coll., Oxford, B.A., M.A., Ph.D.; fellow Magdalen Coll., 1949-; prof. Near Eastern and European Prehistoric Archaeology Oxford U., 1964-; created Knight, 1977. Participated in more than 30 major archaeological expeditions. Author publications, including: What Not to Do in Archaeology, 1960; What to Do in Archaeology, 1970; also numerous excavation and field reports. Clubs: Old Wykehamists, Athenaeum, Wine-tasters, University.

SPRING, PENELOPE ATHENE, anthropologist; b. Cambridge, Mass., May 16, 1928; d. Marcus and Muriel (Snow) Thayer; B.A., M.A., Radcliffe Coll.; Ph.D., Columbia U.; m. Arthur Upton Spring, June 24, 1953 (dec.); 1 son, Alexander Marcus. Lectr. anthropology Oxford U., 1958-68; Mathieson Reader in anthropology Oxford U., 1969-; fellow St. Anne's Coll., Oxford, 1969-. Field work in the Marquesas, East and South Africa, Uzbekistan, India, and among the Pueblo, Apache, Crow and Fox Indians. Author: Sex in the South Pacific, 1957; The Position of Women in Pastoral Societies, 1962; And Must They Die? — A Study of the American Indian, 1965; Caste and Change, 1968; Moslem Women, 1970; Crafts and Culture, 1972; The American Indian in the Twentieth Century, 1974; Hunter vs. Farmer, 1976.

CHAPTER I

Penny Spring was in a blue mood as she scuttled at an undignified pace across Boston Common. It was a mood not helped by the sharp northeast wind that cut through her coat and stirred up the leaves, already fallen and sere, that rustled under her scurrying feet. It was a wind of portent, a harbinger of winter among the fading colors of autumn, and since Penny was feeling very autumnal it brought her no cheer.

The trip to Boston, she reflected, had been a definite mistake. The anthropological conference at Philadelphia had been fun, as had also been her visit with her son Alexander, now in his third year of medicine at Johns Hopkins, but this return to her native heath, and particularly to her alma mater at Radcliffe, had been a mistake, a grave mistake. Among the swarms of the hearty and the young in surroundings that were changed yet which held such tantalizing remembrances of things past, she had felt herself a dumpy and insignificant, middle-aged, mouse-colored ghost.

Seeing her old home in Cambridge with its memories of her delightfully vague archaeologist father and her (mercifully) practical mother had not helped either. She had never rid herself of twinges of guilt for not being the tall, willowy Grecian maiden of her romantic father's dreams—but there was not much to be done about that when one was five-foot-one, plumpish, and with a face like an intelligent monkey's. Though her success in the anthropological field would no doubt have delighted his expert's heart, she nonetheless felt that somehow she had failed him.

After this visit to her publisher—which had become something of a ritual—she would be glad to get out of Boston with its reminders of far-fled youth, glad to get back to Oxford and her partner in crime, Toby.

7

She gained the upper edge of the Common and stood, puffing slightly, in front of the gold-domed State House before turning right and starting her walk along Beacon Street. I really must go on a diet, she thought; it was a promise she made to herself with great regularity and never did anything about. She crossed Tremont Street, firmly avoided the temptations of Goodspeed's antique windows, with their alluring display of old books and prints, and ducked into an equally old-fashioned doorway next door that bore, as it had done for a hundred years, a discreet sign in sober black and white, "Cosby & Son, Publishers." Once inside she relaxed a little; here was a warm familiar milieu, redolent of the smells of paper and ink, cluttered and old-fashioned, but with a warmth that went beyond the mechanical warmth of the steam heat. Cosby's had put out her first slim volume when she was still an undergraduate at Radcliffe and had been her publishers ever since. Some of her books, like *Sex in the South Pacific,* had been smash successes; others, like *The Position of Women in Pastoral Societies,* unmitigated disasters, but throughout Cosby's had stuck solidly by her and to them she always thankfully returned as a familiar landmark in an everchanging world.

The faces in the outer office were all strange to her, but when she gave her name a willowy young blonde leaped out of her chair and assured her, "Mr. Everett has been expecting you, Dr. Spring, and would you please go right in."

John Everett came out from behind his large mahogany desk, hands outstretched to greet her. "Good to see you, Penny, my dear," he chirruped. "Come and sit down. How about a slug of something to keep the cold out? Sherry or brandy? My, you're looking down in the dumps! Anything I can do?" He had ever been a round, jovial little man, whom the years had made even rounder and more amiably philosophic, though he had never lost his youthful avid curiosity about life.

Penny accepted a sherry gratefully. "Oh, it's nothing serious," she reassured him, "but who was it said, 'Never go back'? I've just been to Radcliffe for a couple of days and that was a *bad* mistake. Now I'm just anxious to get back to Oxford and the old familiar faces, where the cult of Youth is not quite so pronounced."

John Everett gave a gentle snort of disapproval. He had never liked her self-imposed exile, albeit it was an exile to one of the world's prestigious universities. He knew full well she had turned down many offers of full professorships at good American colleges, preferring instead the relatively humble lectureship she held in Oxford, and this had always irked him. He had never understood that it had given her the exact measure of security and freedom she wanted; security to bring up her fatherless son and freedom to go dashing off to do whatever fieldwork struck her soaring fancy. Since she had done it all well she was consequently better known in her small world than the majority, ranking right beside other greats like Margaret Mead. "Goodness me! With all the new kudos you got out of that Turkish affair, on top of all the rest of your honored activities, I should think you'd be sitting on top of the world," he chided. "It made quite a stir over here— was in all the Boston papers: 'Famed Boston Anthropologist Breaks Turkish Crime Ring, etc. etc.' Did I send you the clippings? Good for your sales too—we had quite a lot of fan mail coming in for you, most of which I've sent on— oh, all except this"—he picked up a white envelope from his desk—"it only came yesterday and I knew you'd be in, so in view of what's on it I thought I'd better give it to you directly."

Penny took the envelope which bore on it in rather shaky block capitals, URGENT & PERSONAL—DELIVER IMMEDIATELY. The handwriting of the address was unfamiliar to her. "Hmm, obviously someone in a hurry—looks as if I'd better read it now," she observed.

"Go ahead!" John Everett's eyes were gleaming with curiosity.

She opened the envelope and started to read the strange, spiky hand. "My dear Penny," it began: "In view of what we once meant to one another I implore you to help me in a very delicate matter that has just come up . . ." Her eyebrows shot up and she skipped hastily to the signature— the name at the end meant absolutely nothing to her. Her eyebrows went even farther toward her hairline. "Good heavens!" she muttered, and went back to the text. ". . . I can turn to no one I can trust but you," it went on, "and knowing you have had some experience in these matters, having read of the affair at Pergama, I beg you to come down here as soon as possible. It is a matter of the utmost urgency and importance, so I implore you not to fail me. Directions on how to find me are enclosed on a separate sheet. Please, please, *help* me! Your devoted, Zebediah Grange. P.S. I know *all* about you."

"Well, of all the extraordinary things!" Penny murmured in dazed disbelief as she reread it.

"What *is* it?" John Everett was almost bouncing from one round buttock to another with curiosity.

Numbly Penny handed the letter to him. "See what you make of it. It's a call for help from someone I don't even remember . . ." Suddenly, before her mind's eye, danced the vision of braided silk buttons on an old-fashioned tuxedo and the faint smell of mothballs. "No—wait a minute! Zebediah Grange—I do remember something! Good heavens! *Him!*"

"Who?" Everett squeaked, but further explanation was cut off by the sudden shrilling of the telephone. With a cluck of annoyance he took up the phone. "I told you not to disturb me while Dr. Spring was here," he barked into it, then listened. "Oh, I see. It's for you"—he turned to Penny—"your son calling from Baltimore."

"Alexander? What on earth . . ." Penny took the phone. "Alex, are you all right?—You received what!—Read it then.—Good Lord!—Yes, I've got something here from the same man.—Yours says a matter of life and death? Well, I'll look into it, nothing to worry about. Good luck on the exam." She cradled the phone and looked blankly at Everett. "Curiouser and curiouser—he sent a telegram to me care of Alex saying the same thing. He must be desperate."

"Yes but who . . ." Everett started to say when the phone shrilled again and he snatched it up in a fury. "Good God, what is it *now!* Oh, another call for Dr. Spring? Harvard this time . . ." He handed the phone to her, looking as if he might burst with frustration.

"Joe?—Oh, an urgent telegram?—Yes, I see. Well, read it.—Yes, well I've got something here from the same man. —No, I don't know what it's about, but I'll tell you about it later. Thanks for letting me know." She handed the phone back to Everett, who carefully left it on his desk off the hook. "That was the professor of anthropology at Harvard," she explained, "he . . ."

"To heck with him," he fumed. "What about this Zebediah Grange?"

"That's what is so extraordinary," Penny said with maddening slowness, "I haven't seen or heard of Zebediah for thirty years! Not since I was a student in fact. I scarcely remember him at all."

" 'In view of all we meant to one another . . . I know all about you . . .' " John Everett quoted. "Come on! You must remember him better than that!"

Penny's monkeylike little face screwed up in an agony of thought. "I remember he was a student at MIT—engineering I think it was—a couple of years ahead of me. Very keen on archaeology too. Very serious and intense—and shy. He *did* have a sort of crush on me, come to think of it, but we only dated a few times . . ." She trailed off lamely. "Honestly, it was all so long ago . . ." She pulled the sheet of instructions toward her. "Masuit? I don't even know where that is."

"Cape Cod," Everett volunteered promptly.

"We used to summer at Chatham on the Cape, but I don't recall Masuit at all . . . I must be losing my mind." Her tone was worried.

"It's the eighth village of Barnstable—the one no one ever remembers, mainly because it's so small and is almost all one privately owned estate," Everett informed her with a trace of smugness. "It's between Sandwich and West Barnstable. I have a summer place at Sandwich," he explained. Then, "Are you going to see him?"

"It's all so odd," Penny fussed, "I mean he doesn't even give a phone number."

"Probably hasn't got one."

"In this day and age? And look how weird it is. He gives detailed instructions on how to get to Masuit and then says, 'Go to Chase's Variety Store on Kings Highway'—that's 6A isn't it?—'and tell them who you are. They will see that you find me.' Why doesn't he tell me how to get to his house?"

"Maybe he's hiding out," Everett said with enthusiasm. "What do you think it is—murder or drug smuggling?"

"Why should it be either? Heavens, John, you seem to

be enjoying this!" Penny snapped. "He sounds like a first-class nut to *me*."

"Well, I must confess I *am* rather enjoying it," John said with a sigh of satisfaction. "It's not every day in the dull life of a publisher that a mysterious cry for help comes across his desk. As to the nut part . . . I wonder. I can see a nut sending one letter, but two telegrams as well? I mean he obviously is desperate to contact you no matter what the reason. You could take my car," he added craftily. "In fact I could come too to show you the way and see if it's on the up and up." He flipped over his desk calendar and his face fell. "Oh damn, no I can't either. I have a best-selling author coming in this morning—a regular gold mine, but she's *such* a bore, unfortunately a very important bore, so I can't get out of it."

"I'm booked on tonight's TWA flight out of Logan," Penny said doubtfully, "and I've no intention of missing it." But the more she thought about the situation, the more intriguing it seemed.

Everett looked at his watch. "It's still early—you'd have plenty of time to get to the Cape and back, and if it would help I could have someone here get your things from the hotel and take them out to the airport for you and you could leave my car there . . ."

Penny was weakening fast. The trip to the Cape for a mysterious rendezvous with an old beau—no matter how ill-remembered—somehow seemed a far more alluring prospect than her plan of an early lunch and a trip to the familiar wonders of the Boston Museum of Fine Arts, which was how she had proposed to kill the hours until plane time. "Well, I don't know . . ." she began doubtfully.

John Everett cinched the matter. "*I* don't know how you can resist it," he said stoutly. "When you came in here you were down in the mouth and dragging. Now look at you! There's the old gleam of battle in your eye and, by the looks of it, a brand-new mystery on your hands. Why not look into it? What have you got to lose?"

"All right," she said with a sudden grin, "you talked me into it—and be it on your head! Even if it's a wild-goose chase I guess it beats getting fallen arches in the MFA."

Penny was anticipating something sober and impressive like a Lincoln or a Mercedes from John Everett for her foray to the Cape, but she should have known better than to expect the obvious from a Boston Brahmin. She was consequently totally unprepared and somewhat shocked by the jaunty little bright green Triumph Spitfire that stood puffing gently to itself outside the sober doorway of Cosby & Son. With some difficulty John Everett extricated his roundness from the driver's seat. "She's all yours," he announced with the pride of a new father, then with a hint of anxiety, "I suppose you can still manage a clutch drive?"

"Of course." Penny's loftiness of tone masked her raging inward doubts as she crawled into the low front seat. She found she was gazing straight up at a patch of gray sky and the dome of the State House. "It's like driving lying on one's back," she said peevishly.

"I'll adjust the seat," Everett said in a comforting tone. She crawled out again and he fiddled around with levers. "Now try it." This time she could at least see the road. "I'd forgotten you were so small," he said reproachfully. "Wait, I'll get you a cushion." He rushed back in and emerging with one from an office chair managed to insert it under her. "Better?" he encouraged.

Penny nodded and, perched rather insecurely on her new eminence, waved him farewell and edged timorously out into the Boston traffic. John Everett watched her out of sight with the forlorn air of a small boy kept in after school.

Getting the hang of the gears and avoiding being mashed by Boston's madder drivers kept Penny fully occupied until she was on Route 3 heading toward the Cape. The gaily painted storage tanks of Boston Gas signaled the end of anything interesting to look at. The traffic thinned after the Quincy turn off and, as Route 3 began its unending monotony of scrub pine and swamp, she relaxed a little and got down to the business at hand: what *did* she remember of Zebediah Grange?

He was tall—that she vividly recalled, for he had squired her to some college dances and her nose had reached his middle vest button. Tall and gangly, raw-boned, big-handed, with a sort of raw and craggy face to match

the body; the face floated in at the edge of her mind
and out again—it had a shock of black wiry hair trimmed
into a severe crew cut. The main thing she could remember
was his intensity; he had been so intense about archaeology
and about her, but now she could no longer bring to
mind whether he had been intense about archaeology
because of her or intense about *her* because she was his
only link with the strange world of archaeology. She did
recall with a faint twinge of guilt that the urbane Arthur
Spring—who had ultimately become her husband—had
swum into her ken about this time and that she had
dumped Zebediah, albeit as gently as possible, for the
young anthropologist. Zebediah had hung on for some
time after that, though, like a gawky ghost unwilling to
accept his dismissal; and it was only with his graduation
that she had been finally freed of the haunting reproach of
his presence. Basically unlovable as the poor lad had been,
what would he be now, she wondered.

The graceful span of the Sagamore Bridge soared before
her, and she was up and over it and zooming on to the
mid-Cape highway before her punctual stomach reminded
her that it was high time for lunch. "Damn!" she muttered, "I should have stopped for a bite at the circle. I
don't suppose they've built any restaurants yet on the mid-
Cape." She looked hopefully around, but only the serried
ranks of scrub oak and pine raced by her on both sides.
The coziness of the Cape closed around her, and she felt
the odd sense of security well known to all dwellers on
this man-made island. It was not the only thing that closed
around her, for, rolling in from the Massachusetts Bay
side, came a sea fog, obliterating all but the nearest rank
of trees and settling in the hollows of the road like strands
of white cotton wool. She restrained the pace of the eager
little car and began to peer through the thickening mist;
her stomach growled at her warningly. "Oh, dear!" she
lamented, "I really could have done without this. I wonder if there's a restaurant in Masuit. I wonder if I'll even
find Masuit."

She searched anxiously through the mist for the sign
that a hasty glance at Zebediah's strange instructions informed her should be fast appearing. It loomed large and
green at her on the right and she had to brake abruptly to

make the sharp turn off on to Quaker Meeting House Road. The road beyond was narrow and twisty, and she went even slower until the welcome sign for 6A swam whitely out of the mist. "Turn right for two miles," she murmured automatically to herself, and crept forward hunched over the steering wheel like a mouse-colored vulture. A gaggle of white frame houses appeared out of the mist to her right, then suddenly gas pumps and a store to her left. "Chase's Variety Store," she announced in triumph. "I made it! Zebediah, here I come, wherever you are!"

CHAPTER 2

Inside the store a large, broad-shouldered man with a heavy-jowled, doleful face stood stolidly behind the cash register. At the sight of him Penny was overwhelmed by a new wave of shyness about her strange errand. "I wonder if you could help me," she began hesitantly. "My name is Penelope Spring and I'm looking for the house of Zebediah Grange. Could you direct me there, please?"

The dark brown eyes opened a shade wider under the heavy lids, but there was no change in the sad, basset-hound-like expression. "Oh, yes," he growled in a deep voice, "he's been expecting you. Al—bert!" The sudden stentorian roar made Penny jump backward like a startled fawn, but it was immediate in its results. A tow-headed, long-haired youth stuck his head through a side door. "Yes?"

"The lady for Zeb Grange—would you take her down?"

"Oh . . . O.K. This green car yours?" the young man demanded with sudden interest, and the head disappeared.

Penny's stomach gave her a reminding growl. "Just a minute!" she called anxiously; then to the large man, "Really, I did not mean to trouble you—if you'd just tell me the way."

"You'd never find it," he said in a comforting voice. "Albert'll have you there in a jiffy."

Her eyes roved desperately around the crowded shelves. "Do you have any sandwiches?"

He shook his head. "Could sell you a loaf and some cold cuts though."

A shout came out of the mist. "She coming?"

"Oh, it doesn't matter," Penny muttered. She grabbed up a bag of potato chips and a packet of Twinkies from the counter. "I'll just take these, and thank you very much." She paid and scurried out to find the youth already en-

16

sconced in the driver's seat of Everett's car, an expression of near rapture on the young, pimply face.

"Hop in," he urged, and, when she had, gunned the engine and took off at a speed that almost took her breath away. She crammed a Twinkie into her mouth to calm herself and offered one to her chauffeur with mute appeal. "Bad for my acne," he shouted cheerfully over the roar of the engine and zoomed left onto a narrow strip of tarmac, where they bumped over some old railroad tracks. There was water on both sides of them now. "Is that the Bay?" Penny choked through a mouthful of Twinkie.

"No, the cranberry bogs. Flooded 'em early this year. It's going to be a terrible winter, they say," he roared gleefully as he shifted to a higher gear and screamed off the tarmac onto a dirt road that immediately plunged amid thick trees. They emerged from the trees into a cleared area in the middle of which on a slight rise stood a house that, with the exception of a deep front porch, looked exactly like a barn. "Here we are," said her guide, and brought the car to a shuddering halt.

A sudden thought struck Penny. "How are you going to get back?" He emerged somewhat reluctantly from the front seat. "Oh, I'll walk—it's not far on foot and there's not much doing at the store this time of year." He took a last wistful look at the Triumph. "Nice little car that—well, I'll be seeing you!" and he strode off, his hands in his pockets and whistling jauntily, before Penny could decide whether or not she should offer him a tip. "Thank you very much," she called after his retreating back, and was rewarded by a raised hand, though he did not bother to turn around.

She turned toward the silent, barnlike house, misgivings flooding back to her. A battered Chevy pickup stood to one side of it, and far to the left amid the trees she could make out the faded shingles of what looked like another barn. When the whistling of her guide had died away there was an absolute silence in the glade; not the chirp of a bird or the rustle of a leaf disturbed the silent blanketing of the mist. Suddenly the front door of the house opened with the sound of a pistol shot and a tall figure stood framed in it. "Thank God you've come, thank God!" it said, and there was a quaver in the harsh voice.

Zebediah Grange came slowly out onto the deep porch and Penny saw with something akin to horror that the tall figure of her remembrance had been pinched and mangled as if in some giant vise; the whole of the left side was crushed and diminished. His left leg dragged as he walked, and as he came toward her she saw with a qualm of revulsion that his left arm ended in a hook. His hair was still wiry but was a grizzled white, and the face beneath it was weather-beaten and seamed by deep lines that bespoke a life lived in the open. He towered over her and the dark eyes burned down with the same remembered intensity, but in their depths Penny saw emotions which again sent prickles of unease racing up and down her spine; she saw fear there, and the glazed, abstracted look of a man almost at his wit's end.

"I came as soon as I got your message," she said lamely. "You sounded so urgent. What's wrong, Zebediah?"

He appeared not to hear but seized her hand with his good right one in a bone-crushing grip. "I'll get a spade and we'll go right to the site," he said. "I can explain nothing until you have seen for yourself."

Penny felt it was time to assert herself. "Now, look, Zeb, I've just had a long drive down from Boston, I've missed my lunch, I need a drink, and I need to use your bathroom. So, first things first!"

He frowned. "There is no alcohol in the house, I do not drink—but come along!" There was an edge of impatience on the rasping voice.

"Coffee'd be fine," she persisted, as she followed him across the porch into the narrow hallway. The first thing she saw on the hall table was a telephone and her sense of exasperated puzzlement grew. "The bathroom is there"—he indicated a door under the stairway that ran up to the left of the hall—"I'll go put some water on," and scurried with his crablike gait into the small dining room that lay at the end of the hallway.

Penny freshened up and emerged, still wondering to herself why he had gone through all the rigmarole of the telegrams when a simple telephone call would have sufficed. "Where are you?" she called. A muffled shout came from beyond the dining room and she went through it to see him standing before the stove in a small, square kitchen to the right. "Be right with you!" he trumpeted. He emerged with a small jar of instant coffee, a carton of milk, a sugar bowl and the steaming kettle. A single mug stood on the dining room table, and he plonked the rest beside it. "Help yourself," he said ungraciously.

She sat down, feeling uncomfortable, made the coffee and groped for another Twinkie. "Won't you join me?" she offered, trying not to sound sarcastic. Again he shook his head impatiently and shuffled up and down the room. With a mental shrug she took a sip of the scalding coffee—the Twinkies had given her a fierce thirst. "Well now, what *is* this all about?" she said, trying not to look at the hook on his shattered arm, which he was now flexing up and down in a curious manner.

"It must wait until you see for yourself," he rasped. "As soon as you're finished we will go to the site I've been excavating."

"You mean this is something to do with archaeology?" She could hardly believe her ears.

He ignored her question but seized a picture from the top of an old-fashioned tallboy and thrust it toward her. "What does the name Rinaldo Dimola mean to you?" he asked hoarsely.

It did not mean a thing to Penny, but she felt something was expected of her. "Mafia?" she hazarded.

A look of offended rage suffused the weather-beaten face and he seemed to swell. "Certainly not" he rapped. "Rinaldo Dimola is one of the great engineers, one of the great *men* of our time. This is Dimola land you're on, he owns most of Masuit. Dimola Enterprises is one of the great conglomerates of America—surely you must have heard of it!" He sounded outraged. *"This* is Rinaldo Dimola"—he thrust the photo into her hands—"who not only saved my life at the accident but has been my savior ever since. I owe everything I have and am to him."

As he rhapsodized on about Dimola and his exploits Penny dutifully gazed at the picture, which showed two grinning men in the hard hats of construction workers. The one on the left was a younger Zeb, the one on the right obviously Rinaldo: a big man, as tall as Zeb but broad and burly, the arm around Zeb's shoulder like a young oak tree; a broad strong face that seemed vaguely familiar to her, the grin somewhat wolfish, due, she supposed, to the "wolf" canine which showed prominently in the picture on the left side of his mouth and which gave the whole face a predatory look. She could well believe that Dimola was a man to be reckoned with and a man who had created a multi-million-dollar empire.

Since Zeb showed no sign of slackening his paean of praise, she hastily helped herself to another cup of coffee and tried to follow his tangled narrative. A feeling of pity for him welled up in her as he talked of the accident: a bulldozer had crushed him in a gravel slide and Dimola had pulled him free. "He wouldn't let them take my leg—he fought them all, the doctors, everyone, but he couldn't save my arm. Not but what he got me the best artificial one money can buy," he added with pride. The spate suddenly dried up. "You ready yet?" he said roughly.

"Oh yes." She jumped up and followed his shambling form out to the pickup, in the back of which she saw a jumble of digging tools. They set off on the same dirt track she had come in on, but about half a mile into the trees turned left on a still narrower and bumpier one. Zeb had lapsed into a brooding silence, which further irritated Penny; for a man who had been so desperate to get hold of her he certainly was not acting very pleased to see her, so she felt a further explanation was due. "You said you knew all about me and yet we've been out of touch for thirty years. How come?" she demanded.

He did not look at her. "Ann Langley."

"Ann! Is she here?" Penny was astounded.

He nodded, not taking his eyes off the road. "Works for Rinaldo at the mansion."

The affair was becoming more bizarre by the minute. Ann Langley had been one of Toby's most promising students just five years ago, and Penny had been very taken with her. Lovely to look at, highly intelligent, very English. Penny remembered she had tried to talk her out of a liaison with an American Rhodes Scholar but had not succeeded, and Ann had disappeared directly after graduation. She had had a couple of Christmas cards from her, then silence —a not unusual state of affairs with old students. But to find her in this unlikely spot! "What *is* this site then?" she demanded, "an Indian Tutankhamen's tomb?"

The pickup ground to a stop before a barbed wire gate which bore a large *No trespassing* sign. Zeb got out and took a spade out of the back of the truck before unlocking the gate. "It's an Indian encampment and burial ground, about three to four hundred years old," he said, "but we've had a bit of trouble with the Indians over it."

"Indian trouble? Here on the Cape!" Penny was incredulous.

"There's a reservation in Mashpee—Wampanoags—and with all this Indian rights business that's been fashionable the past few years they had to put their two cents worth in over this." His tone was bitter. "I've been digging this site by myself for the past ten years, and I've been as careful as anything, but nothing seems to please 'em . . ." He led her into a small valley which was pockmarked with filled-in trenches. "I've been particularly careful about the burials, knowing how the Indians feel—just digging out and recording what's in the burial and filling in again. When I came here just the other day I saw somebody had been at one of the graves—they lie right along that slope there, see—and I thought maybe some damn pot hunter had been sniffing about for relics. It was then that I found it . . ." He gave her a haunted, fearful look. "Sit down somewhere while I dig it out to show you—I won't be long."

"Can't I help?" Penny asked uncomfortably.

"*No!*" The monosyllable almost exploded out of him. "Time enough for that when you see what it is. It's then I'm going to need your help."

She sat down and marveled to herself at the dexterity with which he clipped his hook onto the shaft of the spade, wielding the handle with his right hand and burrowing into the loose earth of the rectangular grave for all the world like a dog going after a bone. How strange he was! He obviously was not poor; the workman's shirt he was wearing was a Hudson Bay wool of the finest quality, the heavy corduroy pants, though faded and work-stained, of good cut and material. Since he paid no further attention to her she turned to her surroundings.

The Indians had known what they were about in choosing this place, she thought. Above the little valley a sharp breeze was now bending the pines and shredding the sea fog into long white strands, but here all was calm, cozy and protected—hidden. Piles of bleached and broken clam, oyster and scallop shells indicated that the dietary tastes of the ancient Cape dwellers were the same as their modern counterparts. Reminded of her own hunger, she opened the packet of potato chips and furtively crunched under cover of the spade's monotonous rhythm, which seemed to be picking up impetus as Zeb descended into the grave.

She tried to visualize the little valley as it had been when it was a busy Indian encampment, but, bored with this after a while, got up stiffly and wandered over toward the open grave. The sound of the spade had stopped and she reached the edge to see Zeb scrabbling frantically at the bottom with his one good hand. She had just a glimpse of a moldering skull, a few beads and an Indian pot before he rose to his feet and shrank back from her with a startled cry. His face was running with sweat and there was stark fear in his eyes. Without a word he scrambled out of the grave and began spading back the earth at a furious pace.

"Zeb, wait! What on earth is the matter? What did you want me to see?"

The fear-crazed eyes turned to hers. "Nothing—it's too late," he panted, and his eyes swept upward, scanning the mist-shrouded trees in panic. Penny felt the fear reach out and touch her and shivered. "In heaven's name!" she cried, "what are you so afraid of, Zeb? I came here to help! Tell me!"

"I can't," he panted. "Not now. It is too dangerous. I should never have brought you here. You must go. Go at once." He flung the spade down in the partially filled grave and seized her by the arm. "I'll take you back to your car and you must get away."

He towed her, despite her protests, back to the pickup and almost hurled her inside; then they sped up to the silent glade, where he forced her into her own car. Penny was so shocked and dazed by his sudden violence that she could scarcely think. When he slammed the door of the Triumph he leaned toward her and hissed, "Go! And don't come back. Forget all this and everything I've said. Forget me. It is the only way." And without another word he scuttled into the house and slammed the door.

Dazedly, Penny found her way back to the main road, but the farther she drove and calm returned the angrier she grew. By the time she reached Logan airport she was almost apoplectic with fury. She was still boiling when she phoned John Everett to tell him where to pick up the Triumph, and to his anxious inquiry she snarled, "It was a complete waste of my time and your gas. The man was as mad as a hatter."

But when her terror died the puzzlement returned. What on earth was it all about? She would simply have to talk it all over with Toby.

"Talking it over with Toby" had been one of the chief joys and supports of her life for the past twenty-odd years. Tobias Glendower, now Sir Tobias Glendower, unlike Penny, had not been born to the academic world—he had taken refuge in it. Son of a millionaire industrialist father whose overpowering personality and dominating interests had left a permanent mark on those about him, Toby had escaped into the world of the past where he was completely happy. He was brilliant, very eccentric, and undoubtedly drank too much, but all these things the world readily forgave because he was also so very rich. He got on well enough with his fellow man but had a profound suspicion of the female of the species—with one exception: Penny. Their inseparability was one of the continuing themes of wonder and speculation among the student body of Oxford; and the more irreverent of them, seeing his tall, spindly figure hunching along beside her short, dumpy one, had summed it all up by the affectionate label, "The Long and Short of It All." Separate they were outstanding; together they were formidable.

As soon as Penny got back to Oxford she related the whole odd episode to Toby, who listened intently, his small, knoblike head wreathed in clouds of pungent tobacco smoke. "What do you make of it?" she concluded.

He carefully knocked out his pipe and chuckled. "Well, with the facts at hand, precious little, except for the obvious point that your ex-boyfriend is a first-class eccentric. But from what you've told me I'd say (a) that he expected to find something in that grave that had evidently been removed and (b) that that something was connected with the man to whom he is so fanatically attached—what's his name? Dimola? Whatever it was, I think you are well out of it, Penny, and, knowing your propensity for getting into hot water, my best advice is: forget the whole thing."

"I suppose so," she sighed, but in her heart she had the uneasy feeling that far from being an end the strange encounter had only been a beginning.

CHAPTER 3

Robert Dyke was happy and at peace with the world; following a long spell of unemployment after graduation from
high school and a horrendous winter, this was his first day
on his first job and it was a glorious one. There was warmth
in the March sun, a softness to the breeze that blew in off
Massachusetts Bay, the sky was a cloudless blue and a
million diamonds winked at him from the newly drained
cranberry bogs on either side. He walked along the embankment of the old railroad track with its rusty rails and
rotting ties with gratitude in his heart for the town fathers,
who had revived that perennial hare of railway service to
the Cape and so had decreed yet another feasibility study.
It did not concern Robert Dyke that this current study
probably would be shelved like all the rest. He had been
hired to examine the state of the roadbed of the disused
railroad and, being a very conscientious young man, was
probing the splintered ties with a borrowed probe, noting
the condition of the rusty rails, and diligently writing down
the details of their generally sad state in a little notebook.
Just to be doing *something* at long last was a joy to his
heart, and to be doing it outdoors on a day like this was
very heaven. The breeze ruffled his curly black hair and
touched with gentle fingers the ingenuous, snub-nosed face,
which—to his private despair—looked younger than his
nineteen years. Maybe, he thought, if I do a good enough
job on this, they'll give me a more permanent type job,
something to tide me over until I can save enough to go to
college.

An ear-splitting noise erupted suddenly over his head
and he jumped, his eyes shooting upward to the flying-
saucer-like contraption on a telegraph pole by the side of
the track. The banshee screamed for a minute and died

away with a sobbing wail, and when his pulses had stopped jumping he correctly diagnosed it as the noon whistle for the village of Masuit. Lunchtime! He looked about him for a good spot for his alfresco break; lunch by a babbling brook or, in this case, a babbling irrigation ditch appealed to his budding writer's mind. He would sit by the brook and think great thoughts.

He skittered down the embankment toward the larger bog, cheerfully ignoring the large signs, KEEP OUT—NO HUNTING OR TRESPASSING—DIMOLA ENTERPRISES, on it. When he got down to the stone culvert that allowed the water to run underneath the railway embankment from the other bog, he found a depth of only a few inches, scarcely in the babbling brook category. In addition to this he was on the windward side of the embankment, and the breeze though soft was still chill. It found its way through his old football wind-cheater and his patched blue jeans and cut to the bones of his thin, lanky frame. Changing his mind, he scrambled up the embankment again and down the leeward side to the smaller bog. Here, with a sigh of satisfaction, he unhitched his rucksack and, taking out his sandwiches and thermos, settled himself comfortably against the faint warmth of the stones in the stoutly built culvert. He munched away on his lunch, staring idly at the quietly running water and waited for the great thoughts to come. Something nibbled at his mind: the water on this side of the embankment was a lot deeper than on the other —why should that be?

His curiosity aroused, he tested the water with the probe; it was almost two feet deep. There was a pretty star-shaped green weed floating at the entrance to the dark hole of the drain. He stirred it with his hand. Was this the cause, or was something blocking the drain? Maybe he should put that in his report too. He parted the weed and probed within the dark mouth. The probe struck something solid and then yielded, so that he almost pitched face forward into the water. When he withdrew the probe, there was something sticking to the spike. He brought it closer; it was greenly blanched and rotting, but its shape was unmistakable—it was a human ear. When his shocked mind accepted this fact he turned blindly away and quietly vomited up his lunch into the already contaminated stream . . .

"Good Heavens! What do you make of this?" Penny had just opened a letter out of which had fallen an airline ticket, two newspaper clippings, three $100 bills and a letter. Sir Tobias Glendower, who was hunched over a road map of Italy, merely grunted. She read the clippings and the letter twice with little gasps of horror. "Toby, it's a murder!"

He looked up reluctantly and she thrust the papers at him. "Read them! It's incredible!" MURDERED MAN FOUND IN MASUIT CRANBERRY BOG, ran a headline. "Today the naked and partly decomposed body of an unidentified man was found by a railway worker in a stone culvert of a bog on the Dimola estate in Masuit. The police say that a preliminary examination revealed the man had died of an occipital skull fracture and that his face had been mutilated post-mortem. They have no clues as yet to the victim's identity."

The second clipping was headed, BOG MURDER MYSTERY. "An autopsy performed by the state pathologist reveals that the still unidentified man died of repeated blows to the back of the skull and that the body was subsequently further mutilated by repeated blows to the face. It is estimated from the decomposed state of the body that it was placed in the bog between six and seven months ago. The Masuit bog in which the body was accidentally discovered is the property of Rinaldo Dimola, the still-ailing multimillionaire, who is in residence at his Masuit estate. No member of the Dimola family has been available for comment."

The letter in Zeb's spiky hand read starkly: "Please forgive me and come back. This is a matter of life and death. Vital that you come at once. I will tell you all, but in God's name help me. You can stay with Ann Langley. The same arrangements as before. Tell no one. Zeb."

Toby read, his round blue eyes rounder than usual, his round little mouth pursed in a silent whistle. "Hmph," he said when he had finished, "well, it rather looks as if the missing contents of the grave you saw finally turned up—remarkable!"

"What luck it's vacation time—I wonder if we can get a plane tonight," Penny said excitedly.

"You're *going!* Knowing what happened last time?" Toby looked at her in amazement. "And what do you mean *we?*"

"But, Toby, of course I'm going—it's murder and he needs my help. And I naturally thought, well, that you'd *want . . .*"

"My dear Penny," Toby broke in with heavy emphasis, "I made it quite clear to you after the Pergama affair that once was *quite* enough for me. I have absolutely no intention of haring off unasked to the wilds of America to succor a batty ex-boyfriend of yours. I have planned, as you well know, a perfectly civilized Easter vacation. I'm committed to go and look at Cipoletti's excavation near Bologna and then will potter around Tuscan sites for the rest of the time."

"Not to mention Tuscan vineyards," Penny said with venom.

"That too. I've always enjoyed the Tuscan vintages," he agreed with a certain smugness. "And if you had any sense you'd ignore this and join me, as I fully expected you would. I had it all fixed."

"But he says it's a matter of life and death, and I may need help!" she appealed. "Besides, think of all the American wines you've never even tried, New York state, California—why, they've even got wine from Martha's Vineyard now."

Toby shuddered. "Thank you, but no, I'll defer that pleasure. Count me out, right out!"

"Well I think it's extremely selfish of you, though I don't know why I should expect otherwise, knowing you so well," she snapped.

"And I think it is extremely stupid of you to get involved," he returned. "Frankly *I* think it is most unbecoming for a middle-aged widow like you to go careering off across the Atlantic at the behest of an old beau on an affair which is no conceivable concern of yours and which you are not qualified in any shape, manner or form to handle."

They glared at one another and Penny fumed. "Well, there's no sense in arguing with you about humane considerations when you're in this pigheaded state," and flounced out of the room in a fury. Toby shook his head sadly, sighed, and went back to studying his road map.

On her way to London airport that night she admitted a few qualms of doubt herself. Zeb's actions *were* downright peculiar. Remembering the telephone, she had tried to phone him she was coming, only to be told after much delay by the overseas operator that no such phone existed. Baffled, she had compromised by phoning him a cable as to her flight number and time of arrival, but wondered uneasily again about his absurd passion for secrecy despite the apparent urgency of the situation.

Her unease increased when she got to Boston. She had half expected to see him waiting at the customs barrier, but there was no sign of him and no message waiting for her at the arrivals desk either. Grumpily she rented a car at the airport and commenced the drive to the Cape. The rented car seemed sluggish after the zippy zest of Everett's Triumph, and the journey interminable enough to increase her feeling of gloomy doubt.

Oh well, she comforted herself, even if this is another bust, so long as I'm on this side of the Atlantic I can nip down and have a few days with Alexander—it won't be a dead loss. But by the time she had reached the tiny confines of Masuit and drew up before Chase's Variety Store her apprehensions were once again in full flood.

They were in no way allayed by Mr. Chase, who still stood behind his cash register looking more like a sad basset hound than ever. "Oh," he said lugubriously, "Dr. Spring, isn't it? So you're back again."

"Yes. Did Mr. Grange leave a message for me?"

He considered the question. "No, can't say he did. Was in this morning though to pick up some groceries. Would you be wanting Albert again? 'Cos I'm afraid he's off somewhere . . . Never around when you need him," he added with a doleful sigh.

"No, that's all right, I think I know my way now"— Penny was nettled—"but do you know Ann Langley?"

He nodded and a guarded expression came into his sad eyes. "Well, if she comes in, will you tell her I've arrived and that I'll be at Zeb Grange's?"

"If you say so," he agreed, and looked disapproving.

The Grange house seemed silent and unwelcoming as

Penny drew up in the clearing. As the sound of the engine died away the silence of the woods closed around her and still there was no sign of movement from the house. "Really, this is a bit much!" Penny muttered, and stomping across the porch pressed the button for the bell by the front door. She could hear the faint chime within, but there was no movement in answer. She battered on the door in growing anger; it gave beneath her onslaught and she saw the Yale lock had been snubbed open. The first thing she spotted on the small hall table was her cable, open beside its yellow envelope and standing by the enigmatic telephone. "Zeb!" she called, and went in.

There was a faint thump from one of the upstairs rooms and she went to the staircase and started up it. "Zeb?" A very large orange cat appeared at the head of the stairs, yawned widely at her, and then settled himself with his tail curled tidily around his front paws, watching her with impassive amber eyes. "Where the hell is he?" She skirted the enormous cat and made a hasty survey of the upstairs rooms: the large front room a combined study and Indian museum with glass cases that lined the walls crammed with Indian artifacts; the medium-size back bedroom, obviously Zeb's own; the small room next to the bathroom, equally obviously the spare bedroom and general catchall. Everything was neat, characterless, and slightly depressing. A similar survey of the downstairs rooms revealed the same picture: colorless, neatness and emptiness.

Penny went back out on the front porch and looked about in baffled fury. The large cat, who had accompanied her, catching her hostile mood, looked about him with equal interest to see what was disturbing this strange creature beside him. Then, after scenting the air with twitching whiskers, he started off with a purposeful lope toward the barn just visible in the distance amid the budding foliage. "Why not?" Penny said bitterly, and set out after him. "Maybe he knows where Zeb is."

She had already made up her mind what she was going to do. She was determined to find Zeb and after his cavalier treatment would give him a tongue-lashing of the first order. The nerve of him! To drag her across the Atlantic like this on God knows what fool's errand and then to disappear. Well, enough was enough. After the dressing down she would go back to Boston, spend a few pleasant days in Baltimore with Alex and then join Toby in Italy. So what if she had to eat humble pie. At least Toby wasn't the I-told-you-so kind. As for Zebediah!—"Don't call me, I'll call you," she fumed at the empty air, and tried the door of the barn. It was locked.

The cat had disappeared and Penny walked around the barn looking for a window through which to peer. She reached the front of the building and found herself looking out across a vast flat expanse of purplish red interspersed by the darker slashes of ditches; the barn was perched on the very lip of the cranberry bog. A flash of orange down on the bog to her left caught her eye, and she saw the cat gingerly sniffing at something by a stone culvert. There was a slight rustling in the bushes that edged the bog, and the cat looked up startled, sprang away and was gone in great leaps into the underbrush. A prickle of unease ran up Penny's spine and she found herself holding her breath, but the rustling died away and the calm silence reasserted itself.

"Zeb?" she called tentatively, and looked down to see what the cat had been after. When she saw what it was a cold hand clamped around her heart: a substantial boot, with about an inch of Argyle sock showing above it, was sticking out of a ditch.

She skittered down the bank and hurried, dry-mouthed, to the ditch. Lying on his back, his eyes gazing unseeingly up at the gray March sky through a mask of mud, lay Zebediah Grange, a thin trickle of blood coming from one nostril into the corner of the flaccid mouth. Kneeling down, she tried to wipe away the mud with her handkerchief. His clothes reeked of whisky and there was a smashed whisky bottle at his side. Her other hand groped at his neck for the sign of a pulse. It was there, shallow and thready but definitely there—Zeb was still alive! She put a hand under his head, trying to ease him away from the trickling water in the ditch, and encountered sticky wetness. Drawing the hand away with involuntary repugnance, she saw it was red with blood. All her former fury evaporated in a flash to be replaced by sick realization. Now it was very clear why Zeb Grange had not been on hand to greet her or to reveal what had so tormented him all this weary time. Someone had made a very determined effort to shut his mouth forever.

But they had not quite succeeded, and, by God, if she had anything to do with it, they wouldn't. She leaped to her feet and became aware of a figure staring down at her from the barn, its hands clapped to its mouth, a frail, well-remembered figure with a shining aureole of golden hair.

"Is he dead?" Ann Langley asked with a quaver.

"No! Ann, get hold of yourself," Penny cried. "Go telephone the rescue squad and the police. I'll stay here and do what I can. Someone has just tried to murder Zeb, but, by the grace of God, they have not succeeded, and they *won't!*"

CHAPTER 4

Zeb, like an oversize broken doll, had been loaded into the rescue squad ambulance, which had screamed away to the Cape Cod Hospital in Hyannis. Now a short, stocky man, his muscles bulging under the dark blue uniform of the Barnstable police, was looking at Penny with a very unfriendly expression. "I know it's not easy to keep your head in an emergency, but you shouldn't have moved him," he reproved.

"I didn't!" Penny's tone was indignant. "I only tried to ease his head away from the water and it was then I found someone had tried to bash his head in—after that I didn't touch him."

His eyes narrowed. "Then how come his face was all over mud?"

Her own eyes widened. "Wait!" she cried, and clutched her forehead with a mud-begrimed hand, leaving it streaked like an Indian in war paint. "This doesn't make any sense at all! His attacker obviously left him face down in the bog. *I* didn't turn him over, but somebody else must have before I got here."

"*Two* people? Then why didn't the second one call for help?" His tone was incredulous.

"Maybe whoever it was didn't have time . . ." She told him about the rustling in the bushes and the scared behavior of the cat.

"Mighty funny way for anyone to behave," he muttered dubiously.

"But why should his attacker first try to kill him and then save him from suffocation by turning him over? That would be even stranger."

"To go through his pockets—it's hard to get into a man's pockets when he's lying on his face," the policeman said smugly. "That's how I see it—a simple case of robbery by some hippie or junkie who saw an easy mark in a lonely

33

place. There was nothing in his pockets but some keys, a penknife and a couple of Indian arrowheads—no wallet."

"Just a moment," Penny cried again, as something flashed on her memory screen, "it's not that simple—I'm pretty sure I saw his wallet when I went through the house."

"You were in his house?" His suspicion was marked.

"Well, yes—the door was open, and I just couldn't understand why he wasn't there to meet me, so I looked all over for him. He'd sent for me, you see, and he knew I was coming—the cable I sent was right there in plain sight."

"We'd better get back there then and you can show me," he growled. They trailed back along the dirt track, collecting a pale and shaken Ann Langley into their train. She had almost passed out when she had come back with the rescue squad, and they had hastily ministered to her and left her propped against a tree.

In the house Penny led the way upstairs and pointed mutely to the wallet that stood on the night table beside Zeb's narrow bed. The policeman examined it, his brow furrowed. "It has over a hundred dollars," he said sadly. "Well that certainly seems to rule out robbery; still, "he brightened, "that doesn't mean robbery wasn't the *motive* —the attacker may have been disappointed and then just left him like that."

Something else clicked in Penny's mind. "I'm afraid it's nowhere near that simple," she said slowly, "because unless it has been put away somewhere, there *is* something missing from the house." She led the way downstairs again to the small dining room and pointed to the chest of drawers.

"When I was here last there was a large photo of Mr. Grange with Mr. Dimola on that—in fact, if you look closely you can see where it stood in the dust."

The policeman stared at it and at her. "You were here before?"

"Yes, briefly, last fall. Mr. Grange showed me the picture then."

A light seemed to dawn on him. "What kind of frame was it in?"

"Silver," she said reluctantly.

"Aha!" He was triumphant. "Can you spot anything else missing?"

"I'm afraid apart from that I just wouldn't know." She looked a little helplessly at Ann. "Do you know?"

Ann started out of a reverie and shook her head. "No, I'm sorry, I've only been in here a few times to look at Zeb's Indian collection." The policeman prowled around for a bit, pulling open drawers and examining dusty surfaces while Penny and Ann looked on in silence. "Well," he said, after a while, "it's possible that some sneak thief came in here to lift a few things, that Grange spotted him and chased him on to the bog, they had a fight and that was that. It's a bit early in the year for that kind of thing, but we get it all the time in summer; people on the Cape never have got the hang of keeping their doors locked."

"Maybe I shouldn't say this, but I'm afraid there is a definite link between this attack and the murder you are investigating," Penny said stubbornly.

"What murder?" His face was blank.

"Why, the body in the bog, of course!"

"Oh, that." His face clouded over. "I don't know anything about it. Anyway, what has it got to do with this?"

"I think I can explain, Dr. Spring," Ann Langley put in hastily, seeing the look of outraged disbelief on Penny's face. "You see, when that body was found a state patrol car just happened to be at Mr. Chase's store as the young man came in with the news. The *state* police have been investigating the case. This officer is from the local police."

Penny turned on him. "You mean you don't do it together?"

"Not unless asked," he said, thin-lipped with disapproval. "Anyway what has that got to do with this?"

She hesitated. Her first obligation she felt was to Zeb; what his involvement in all this was she had no idea, but until she could talk to him she felt she had no right to violate the secrecy he had wished. What was more, so far she only had suppositions and no facts to go on. "It was a very private matter for Mr. Grange. We are old friends from college days and he wanted my help on it," she said, "and until we know how he is and I can talk to him I don't think I can say anything further."

"Withholding evidence is a serious offense," the officer snapped.

"I am withholding nothing about *this* case," Penny said firmly, "in fact I've told you all I know."

"Well, tell it again," he said, busy with his notebook, and Penny and then Ann went over the events as he took their statements down. He had them sign the statements, then stood up. "Well, if you think of anything to add, call me at the station. Officer Birnie, Ernie Birnie." He grimaced at the name, which Penny surmised had given him a lot of trouble through life. "You'll be staying on here of course until this is settled?"

Penny glanced at Ann. "Er, yes. I understood from Zeb that he had made arrangements with Miss Langley here."

Ann flushed a little and did not look at her. "Yes, officer, Zeb called on me last night and asked me if I'd be willing to take a lady friend of his as a paying guest for a while. That's why I came over to see him this morning, to ask about the arrangements. He did not tell me it was to be you," she said to Penny, an appeal in her voice. Officer Birnie looked from one to another of them curiously before shutting his notebook with a snap. "So that's where you can be reached if needed?" he asked.

"Yes, at least for the moment." Penny felt confused and awkward.

"O.K. Then you'll be hearing from me." He made his way out, leaving the two women staring at one another in silence.

"Look, Ann, if this isn't convenient for you, I can easily go to a motel," Penny at last said a little desperately. "I had no idea Zeb had been so vague about all this. I feel I must clear this up for his sake, but I don't want to put you out."

The girl looked drained, the gray eyes, which Penny had remembered as sparkling and full of life, sad and haunted. "No, it's not that, I'd like to have you. But . . . well . . . there's a lot I should tell you . . ."

"Good idea," Penny said briskly, "and before you do I think we both could use a good stiff drink and a hearty lunch. Treat's on me. Where's a good place?"

The good place turned out to be a wayside restaurant in Barnstable. When they were finally settled before their drinks Penny, at least, was looking forward to a king-size seafood platter and took a satisfied gulp of her old fashioned. She said encouragingly, "So, Ann, catch me up to date on what you have been up to."

The fair girl toyed with her vodka martini, her eyes downcast. "I scarcely know where to begin—so much has happened . . ."

"The last I heard you'd decided to come over here with your young man—what was his name?—John something or other?"

"John Roberts." Ann's tone was bitter. "And you were right about that setup. It wasn't right, it didn't work out." She gave a deep sigh and Penny kept quiet, she too not being the "I-told-you-so" kind. "I got pregnant and when the baby was born he just walked out on me. Did not want the responsibility." She looked at Penny with miserable eyes. "I have a three-year-old daughter."

"Then that's his loss and your gain," Penny said definitely. "Unless *you* think otherwise. And you have plenty of company these days."

"No, Penny's all the world to me." Ann's fingers tightened on her martini glass and the color flooded up under the fair, translucent skin. "I called her after you; I hope you don't mind."

"I'm very flattered," Penny said, and waited for more.

"I know all they say about the disadvantages to a child brought up by a single parent," Ann said fiercely, "but I'll never give her up, never!"

"My dear, there are a lot more *advantages* to a child brought up by a single loving parent than two *un*-loving ones," Penny said with firmness. "I ought to know. I did it myself. Alex was only two when his father died."

"But that was different—you were married."

"Oh, what does that matter any more! Thank God for Ms.! No one will ever even know unless you tell them."

"And *you've* always had Toby Glendower," Ann blurted out, and then flushed a brilliant scarlet. "Oh! I shouldn't have said that. I'm sorry!"

"Not to worry," Penny said placidly. "It's true Toby has always been around, but actually he's hopeless with children. Alex and he never did see eye to eye, Alex being very much of the twentieth century and Toby never having really got beyond B.C."

Having made one gaffe, Ann plunged on. "We students never could figure out why you two weren't married."

"Us! *Married?*" Penny said with horror. "Oh, no, that would never do!"

"But you are always together!"

"Yes, but only when we *want* to be—that's different. And not always, like now," Penny said with a faint resentment against the absent Toby. "Anyway, enough about me. Back to you and your daughter. How did you end up here?"

Their food arrived, and while Penny tucked into her platter and listened, Ann toyed with hers and talked.

"It was just luck, really. I was flat broke after John left me, and the market for archaeologists with no experience and a newborn baby in tow isn't exactly flourishing. I saw this ad for a live-in research assistant—and it was Steven." Again a hectic flush mantled her fair cheeks, which Penny made a mental note of. "Steven Dimola is a scholar. He's a keen amateur Assyriologist, among other things, and he's done a lot of work. He's really quite good," Ann blurted on. "Anyway, I got the job, and since then I've been a sort of general girl Friday to the Dimolas when they are here. It has worked out very well. They have a Portuguese butler whose wife doesn't work because she has three small children, so she baby-sits Penny while I'm working. It's fine for her because she has lots of playmates, and of course we all live very close together on the estate . . ."

"Talking of living close together," Penny said, glancing at her watch and abandoning her platter with some reluctance, "I think I'd better check the hospital to see how Zeb is. When I tried before they couldn't tell me anything. They said to call back in about an hour."

She returned after a considerable interval to find Ann moodily smoking, her own lunch hardly touched. Penny reapplied herself to hers. "What a runaround," she grimaced, "I had to claim kinship before they'd tell me a thing—not that there's much good to tell. He's in the intensive care unit in a coma—multiple skull fractures. It could go either way. I only hope he's as tough as he looks." She polished off her plate in grim silence, then addressed herself to a luscious chocolate gateau while Ann drank coffee and chain-smoked. Why, thought Penny, if your job is working out that well are you so confoundly nervous, my girl? She had reached the coffee stage herself and was about to open this intimate subject when a burly figure in blue caught her eye. Officer Birnie was advancing purposefully toward them. "Why," he said accusingly as he came up to the table, "didn't you tell me right off you were related to Zeb Grange? We've been trying to locate his next of kin."

"I? To Zeb!" Penny started to protest, when light dawned. "Oh, my! Word certainly does travel fast on the Cape, doesn't it?" She smiled at him weakly. "I suppose you got that from the hospital. Well, er, I'm afraid that was a little white lie. I'm no relation."

He turned a dull purple and seemed to swell. "You mean you *aren't!* After all the trouble I've been to to track you down!"

"Well, you know how difficult hospitals are about giving information," Penny said feebly. "I had to say something to find out about him."

"Then who *is* his next of kin, tell me that!" Birnie demanded in a muffled bellow. "He's such a hermit that no one seems to know the first thing about him or his family."

"I'm afraid I don't know either," she confessed. "You see, apart from that brief visit last fall I told you about I've been out of touch with Zeb since we were in college. I know very little about him."

Birnie looked as if he might burst at any moment, so Ann put in hurriedly, "I think I've heard Zeb mention a nephew who lives on the Cape somewhere—his brother's son, so the name will be the same. Would that help?"

"It might," he growled and after another venomous glance at Penny stalked out.

"Oh, dear, I'm afraid that's rather cooked my goose as far as he is concerned," she exclaimed in some dismay. "I don't know how I manage it, but I always seem to get on the wrong side of the law, and this time there isn't even a Bilger in sight." Ann gazed at her blankly. "Oh, that was a young policeman who helped me in the Pergama affair," Penny explained hurriedly. "I certainly could use him around now. "But let's get back to the Dimolas and the people on the estate."

"You mean normally or now?"

"Is there a difference? Well, start with now and go on to normally."

"Now the whole family is here," Ann said. "There's Rinaldo and his wife Annette, his second wife, that is. And Steven and his wife Inga—she's Swedish . . ." The color rose and ebbed in her cheeks again and Penny felt she had a possible answer to her unasked question. "Then there's Alexander, that's the younger son, and his wife Wanda—she used to be an actress—and Maria Bearse, Rinaldo's only daughter, who is living at home now after her divorce. That's the family. Then there's the servants, six of them, two Portuguese and four Cape Verde Islanders, plus the Italian chef. Some of them live in the house, the others in Masuit."

"And who else lives on the estate?"

"Just Zeb and I."

"And normally?"

"Well, it's a year-round house for Steven and Inga— he can work better here. The six servants are theirs. For the others it's a weekend and summer place. Dimola Enterprises has its HQ in Boston. Rinaldo has his town house on Beacon Hill and brings his Italian chef with him when he visits here. Alexander and his wife also have a house in Wellesley Hills, and Maria normally lives in New York but since the divorce has been living with her father."

"I'm convinced, the more I think of it, that Rinaldo Dimola is the key to this whole thing," Penny said slowly. "The first thing I must do is to talk with him, then perhaps I can begin to make sense of this business."

"I'm afraid that's out of the question." Ann was looking at her oddly.

"How so? He's not another Howard Hughes, is he?"

"Then you don't know?"

"Know what?"

"Last September Rinaldo Dimola was stricken with a massive cerebral hemorrhage. He was paralyzed, and he has not spoken a word since."

CHAPTER 5

"Why would anyone want to steal a photo?" Penny wondered. Her inner dismay at the news of Rinaldo Dimola was mixed with the growing certitude that Zeb's weird behavior was an outgrowth of his fanatical devotion to the stricken multimillionaire and linked to the latter's illness in some way. She had ascertained from Ann that the stroke had occurred only a few days before Zeb's first summons, and that when she had been on the Cape previously the millionaire was still hovering between life and death. Since then his condition had stabilized, and lately he had shown some slight signs of improvement.

"I've no idea—it appears to be so senseless," Ann answered Penny's question. They had retreated to Ann's little cottage in the pines and were now drinking coffee, which Penny noted seemed to be Ann's principal item of diet. The cottage, Ann explained, had been an overflow guest house for the main house. It was a low, shingled Cape Cod rambler with three bedrooms, each with its own bath, a large living-dining room with a huge stone fireplace and a tiny kitchen. The trees clustered closely around the house, making it rather dark, but inside it was cozy and Ann had added a lot of pleasing feminine touches: hanging plants of all kinds, bright cushions on the basic, solid maple furniture, and jazzy modern prints on the pine-paneled walls. After the dreary starkness of Zeb's house Penny found it a comforting relief.

"Dimola isn't one of these tycoons who hates to be photographed, is he?" Penny was groping for answers.

"No, far from it. Up until just after I came to work for them he was very gregarious in a rather heavy-handed sort of way—not so much the past two years though."

"Any reason for that?"

"Not that I know of. But he seemed to undergo a sort of personality change; become much more somber and withdrawn, and even more of a 'padrone' if that were possible. Maybe his stroke was boiling up for a long time."

"Possible, I suppose," Penny murmured. "When I saw that photo I felt his face was so *familiar,* I wish I could remember where I'd seen it."

A faint smile appeared on Ann's face. "Maybe I can help on that." She got up and took a heavy Italian art book off a bookshelf. Opening it, she placed it before Penny. "Is that it, by any chance?" Penny gasped. "Why, of course!" She was looking at Castagno's fresco portrait of the condottiere Niccolò da Tolentino from Florence Cathedral—the resemblance between it and Rinaldo Dimola was striking.

"If ever there was a throwback, Rinaldo is it," Ann went on. "It's remarkable really, because he's a fourth-generation American—his great-grandfather immigrated in the late 1860s—but he is the most complete Italian I've ever seen. Not a *modern* Italian, a Renaissance Italian, perhaps even an ancient Roman. 'La famiglia' is his God, I think —the complete patriarch, the complete autocrat." She was becoming quite animated. "You should see his part of the main house, it's like stepping into the ducal palace in Florence. And I think he sees himself like that, the head of a hereditary empire; only in this case it is a twentieth-century empire he has carved out himself."

"Not the easiest person to live with I should imagine," Penny murmured.

A slight cloud passed over the fair face in front of her. "Well in some ways no, but he wasn't a bully, and he was fair according to his lights—very much the iron hand in the velvet glove. Not that that is always appreciated . . ." She trailed off.

"Tell me about the rest of the family," Penny encouraged. "Are they like him?"

"Alexander is very like his father, both to look at and in character. He's his father's right hand in running the business and has been doing it entirely and very ably since Rinaldo's stroke. Steven's very different, more like his mother, I suppose—she was a Cape Cod Chase. Not the banking Chases but a branch that hung on to most of its land and was pretty well-to-do in a quiet way. All this Masuit land was hers. Anyway, Steven has no liking for business. All his tastes are scholarly or artistic—collecting painting and sculpture, archaeology, genealogy and so on. It was he who got his father all fired up about the Dimola family genealogy—and, by the way, it should be 'D, apostrophe, Imola'—it's a little place some thirty miles south of Bologna in the hills, I believe."

"D'Imola, D'Imola," Penny muttered, "why does that make me think of the poet Dante?"

Ann beamed at her like a proud parent. "That's right," she encouraged, "one of Dante's supporters and early biographers, Benvenuto D'Imola. Rinaldo thinks he's descended from him, though I'm a bit dubious about it myself, and so is Steven, but he is such a gentle soul he doesn't like to disillusion his father."

"Did Rinaldo approve of Steven's activities?"

Ann looked surprised. "Why, yes! Steven's the elder son, and in Rinaldo's way of thinking this means he can do no wrong. Of course money is no object anymore to any of them, but Steven is Rinaldo's successor in every sense of the word. When he dies, the empire is Steven's."

Penny's eyebrows shot up. "And how does Alexander feel about that?"

Ann looked slightly uncomfortable. "Well, he and Steven get along all right, but naturally there's a bit of resentment. Not that Steven would dream of taking over from him. If Rinaldo goes, Alexander in fact *will* run the business."

"But not as its head," Penny murmured thoughtfully. "And what about the daughter?"

"Maria is the family maverick. She and her father don't get on at all well, though I think she's more like him than either of them care to admit. He is so patriarchal as far as women are concerned, it's almost unbelievable, so she's very much the low member on the family totem pole. She's overreacted to this and is one of the most fervent women's libbers I've come across, an absolute fanatic about it. Rinaldo's an ardent Catholic and I swear she has married and divorced twice just to get his goat. A classic love-hate relationship, because she always comes home between husbands—just to fight with her father, I'm certain. *And* she's a born mischief maker. But she must be fond of him because since his stroke she's been a tigress with the others over his medical care. It is she who insisted on bringing in this newest doctor, who really does seem to be doing some good at long last."

"And how does that sit with the second Mrs. Rinaldo Dimola and the rest of the distaff side?"

"It's hard to tell what Annette Dimola thinks about things," Ann confessed. "In a sense she's the odd man out. They haven't been married that long, about five years, I believe, and she is so much younger than he, nearly the same age as Maria. A bit of a mystery woman really and very secretive. I don't quite know what Rinaldo saw in her besides the fact she is young and fairly attractive; she seems, well, so *neutral*. Though she too can be surprisingly strong-willed at times. After the first crisis was past it was she who insisted that the nurses should go and the family care for Rinaldo."

"Isn't that sort of dangerous?" Penny queried.

"Not really. Inga"—Ann's color came up again—"was a trained nurse, and one of the Portuguese servants had been a practical nurse, so with them, Annette, Maria, and occasionally myself all taking turns, he has been well looked after. There's not much that *can* be done, you know, except wait and watch."

"Doesn't Alexander's wife come into this?"

"Wanda? Oh no, she's useless. Can't stand sickness, and is so nervous and up-tight she'd be more trouble than help. An ex-actress who has never got away from the tinsel —*terribly* narcissistic."

The Dimola men, Penny reflected, despite their enormous wealth, did not seem to go in for very high-born or high-powered wives. She voiced part of her thought. "And what does Rinaldo think of his daughters-in-law?"

Ann hesitated. "I think he was a little disappointed when Steven married Inga. But it was a fait accompli and so he accepted it. Steven had gone to the Middle East just after his father's second marriage. He got sick out there, and Inga was a nurse at the hospital he was in. They came back married. Mind you, Inga knows which side her bread is buttered on, she is very shrewd in some ways. She really used to play up to Rinaldo as father-of-them-all, and she is so devoted to and possessive of Steven—well, this in Rinaldo's book makes her a perfect wife." She blushed and looked down. "You see, basically with Rinaldo women really don't *count* for all that much. Wanda's a real pain, but she's extremely decorative and *can* be charming and amusing, so he likes her too. In fact, outwardly he seems to care a lot more for his 'in-laws' than he does for his own daughter."

"And how does Zeb Grange fit into the local and family picture . . ." Penny started to say, when the hidden phone shrilled suddenly, causing them both to jump. It was evidently located in Ann's bedroom, for she excused herself and was gone some time, returning a little pink in the face. "That was Steven," she announced breathlessly. "He has just got back from the hospital. I'm afraid there's no change in Zeb's condition; he's stabilized but still in a deep coma. Steven wanted to know if you would be free to lunch with the family tomorrow. He's very anxious to meet you."

"Well, if that is convenient for you," Penny said doubtfully. She was not at all sure she was ready to face the Dimolas en masse, but realized she would have to do it sooner or later if she was ever to test out her hunch.

"I usually also have lunch there," Ann explained. "It saves time trekking to and from here, and I make it my main meal. I just get a light supper for little Penny and me. I'm not much of a cook," she added, causing the elder woman's gloom to deepen, for if there was one thing she coveted it was three square meals a day.

"Maybe I can help out while I'm here," Penny volunteered quickly. "I'm no gourmet cook but one of the best make-do-and-mend cooks on record. The things I can do with a few cans you wouldn't believe!"

"Oh, really? Yes, that would be nice," Ann said, but there was a faint doubt in her voice. "I've got to go and pick up Penny now. Would you care to come along?"

"Certainly," the elder Penny agreed, "but there's one more thing before we go. Zeb had a telephone and so have you, and yet when he contacted me he never once mentioned it and in fact seemed to go to some pains *not* to use it. When I tried to contact him I was told he wasn't listed. Have you all got unlisted numbers or what?"

Ann shook her head. "It is a bit complicated. You see the phones on the estate all link to the main house. It's a sort of intercom. We *can* get outside numbers on our phones, but it means dialling through the switchboard at the mansion, and the Dimola number is unlisted for obvious reasons. In the old days a security guard used to man it, but recently, since it's situated near the kitchen, usually one of the servants keeps an eye on it. They have a buzzer system."

Penny thought about that. A possible solution to Zeb's caginess came to her. "And, presumably, like most switchboards it has a listening device?" Ann nodded. "I see."

So Zeb had been unwilling to have anyone know about his attempts to contact her or to know about her visits. Why? Shyness about his personal affairs? Or because he did not trust one or more persons in that mansion and wanted to keep the knowledge from them? "When Zeb asked you about putting me up was it over the intercom?" she asked.

"No, he came here."

"Was that usual?"

"Not very." Again Ann looked uncomfortable. "Zeb was such a private sort of man, he rarely visited around. I was surprised when I saw him at the door, and he wouldn't even come in. He was terribly vague too—no names, no times—nothing."

"Did he seem nervous?"

"No. Worried, perhaps, but not nervous."

"I asked them in England to phone my cable, but if the number is unlisted could they have done that?"

Ann shrugged. "I don't think so—not unless Western Union had it. They would just send it along by messenger."

"And where would it go? Direct to Zeb or to the mansion?"

"To the mansion, and then the servants usually deliver it around."

"So someone at the main house could have seen the cable?"

"Possibly."

"That's something I'll have to check." Penny was thoughtful. "Oh dear, I wish I knew a little more about all this. I feel as if I'm groping in a thick fog."

"If there's anything I can do to help . . . and Steven is very worried too. He likes Zeb very much."

"Thank you, my dear, I may need your help badly before

I'm finished." Penny sighed as Ann gazed at her with troubled eyes.

They drove the short distance into Masuit and picked up the young Penny, who was a miniature version of her mother and whose fairness stood out in the small swarm of dark-haired, dark-eyed infants that clustered around the skirts of the evidently curious Mrs. Mendoza.

Ann became much more animated and much more her former self in the company of her small daughter. Penny watched them laughing and playing together with a stirring of pity in her heart. It seemed rather painfully obvious to her that, emotionally speaking, Ann had proceeded from the frying pan into the fire. Steve Dimola may have been Ann's rescuer from desertion and penury, but he appeared to have captured her heart as well—and he was very much a married man in a Catholic and conservative family. She wondered how he felt about it and found herself anticipating the morrow with misgivings.

After an insubstantial supper, which added to her dejection, jet lag began to catch up on Penny. "If you don't mind," she said after a huge yawn, "I think I'll turn in. I really will have to get busy tomorrow, and what with all the excitement and the time change I'm beat."

When she was finally abed in the small, cozy guest room, all the coffee she had consumed caught up with her, and, despite her tiredness, she found her mind ticking relentlessly. She gazed at the paneled walls with their bright prints, waiting for drowsiness to come, while outside the clustering pines whispered their secrets to the chill March night. Despairing of sleep, she sat up in bed, munched on a chocolate bar she had providentially supplied herself with, and tried to put order in her jumbled thoughts: (a) Zeb had had something urgent to tell her about the body in the bog—check the body. (b) Someone had silenced him before he could pass that something on. (c) The someone had known she was on her way, so must have seen the cable—check cable. (d) The someone had not finished off the accident/murder—why? Disturbed? Second party? Who had turned the body over? (e) Why had the photograph been stolen?

In a swirling kaleidoscope she saw the wolfish smile of Rinaldo Dimola as, clad in the armor of a condottiere and mounted on a battle charger, he paced toward her. "My family is my God," he informed her. Zeb walked by his side, his hand on a stirrup, gazing devotedly up into his face. "I would give up my life for you," Zeb declared.

She slipped down in the bed, as the first waves of sleep lapped over her, but as she drifted off another disturbing vision came to her: a fair girl, eyes wide with terror, exclaiming, "Is he dead?" Not "What's happened?" not "Is he hurt?" just "Is he dead?" Now *that,* thought Penny, is queer, very queer indeed; and she slept.

CHAPTER 6

"John, I need help." Penny's tone was exasperated. "I've tried every which way to get the state police to let me see the body or at least a copy of the autopsy report and have gotten nowhere. And time is running out on it because the inquest is tomorrow and after that they intend to bury him, in spite of the fact he is still unidentified. Also—since Heaven knows how long I'll have to stay—I may have to have some cash advance on my royalties."

"No problem on that last matter, and I'll see what can be done on the other." John Everett's naturally exuberant curiosity was overlaid by a certain uneasiness. "But, Penny, in view of what you told me last night on the phone, do you think you ought to get involved in this? I mean, if your suspicions are correct and someone tried to silence Zebediah Grange before he could talk to you, you could be in some danger yourself. Why not leave it to the police?"

"Because, so far, both the state *and* the local police don't seem to believe a word I've said. They refuse even to consider a link between the two, even though I've shown them Zeb's letters and told them what little I know. Things aren't helped by the fact that the murder is the state police's baby and the attack on Zeb belongs to the local police, and they don't appear to communicate too well. My own case isn't aided by the complete dearth of concrete evidence or by Zeb's being recognized locally as such an eccentric character. Also the possible involvement with the Dimolas doesn't help either. I mentioned to the state detective in charge of the case—a Detective Eldredge—that I thought it was in some way connected with Rinaldo Dimola, and he shut up like a clam. I don't know whether it was because *he* knew something I don't, or whether the very name of Dimola is too powerful in these parts to be considered. So do you think you can pull any local strings to loosen them up a bit? I really would appreciate it."

John Everett sighed slightly on the other end of the phone. He knew Penny well enough to realize that she had the bit firmly between her teeth and would therefore be immune to sweet reason. "I'll see what I can do and call you back as soon as possible," he said. "I may be able to manage something with the state police but I don't carry any clout in Barnstable. Where can I reach you?"

"I'm calling from a phone booth at Chase's Variety Store in Masuit," Penny explained, "but you could call me at the Langley cottage." She gave the private Dimola number and the extension and added, "And don't say too much because, unless Zeb was completely paranoid, there is a strong possibility that there's a listening post in the Dimola house. It's a funny setup."

This did nothing to soothe John Everett's fears, "Well, for God's sake be careful!" he said, and rang off.

Penny emerged from the booth to find she had an audience. Mr. Chase was standing at the door of his store and Albert was peering under the hood of her car. "Bad business about Zeb," remarked Mr. Chase, his long face more lugubrious than ever. "I hear you were the one who found him . . ." he invited.

She did not want to be involved in a long explanation, so she cut him off. "Yes—and I must get over to the hospital to see him. What are you *doing*, Albert?"

The towhead emerged from the hood. "What happened to the Triumph?" Albert asked sadly. "This one is a real clunker. Want me to try and rev it up a bit?" He looked as if he was nursing a powerful hangover.

"No, thank you," Penny said hurriedly, "it's a rental car, and it's fine for now." As she drove back to the cottage Albert's hung-over state called to mind another curious fact she would have to look into. Zeb had reeked of whisky when she had knelt over him, and there had been a smashed whisky bottle by his right hand. And yet, when she had talked to the local police, neither Officer Birnie nor Detective Thompson, who was now in charge of the case, had made a single mention of this fact. Her active imagination chewed on this. She recalled vividly Zeb's strong negative reaction to her own demand for a drink; it could have been the reaction of a fanatic teetotaler *or* of an ex-alcoholic. This was something else she would have to check. If it were the latter, the silence of the local police was understandable—they were not going to point the finger at a local man who had fallen off the wagon. And yet, if this were the reason, they were doing Zeb a disservice and had failed to make an observation she herself had made. As she had swabbed his face and listened to his labored breathing, her head almost touching his mouth, there had not been a trace of alcohol on his breath—it had all been on his clothes.

An ugly picture of the would-be murderer rose before her; the swift savage blow from behind that had sent Zeb toppling into the ditch by the culvert, then a hasty setting of the scene, the bottle smashed and poured on him, a stone of the culvert smeared with blood and hairs—the setting of a fatal accident for a drunk. And yet the scenario had not been completed—*someone* had interrupted, someone had turned Zeb over on his back before he choked to death in the mud of a ditch. But who and why? And had that someone seen the would-be killer?

She dulled her impatient waiting by writing a long letter to Toby detailing all that had happened so far, and was still engrossed in this when the telephone shrilled and proved to be John Everett, announcing the success of his mission with all the pompous assurance of his Brahmin ancestry.

His news sent her hurrying to Hyannis and to the funeral home in which the body had been held since the autopsy. Here she was greeted by a very young man, whose cheerful countenance belied his mournful trade. He shook hands vigorously and introduced himself. "Dave Baxter, Dr. Spring. My father, Tom, and John Everett went to Harvard together. Er, this is all a bit irregular," he confided, "and I'd appreciate it if you didn't divulge where your information comes from, but, since Dad and Mr. Everett are such great friends, I'll try and tell you anything I can."

"May I see the body?" Penny asked eagerly.

"No, I'm afraid I can't go that far, and, besides, I'm afraid you'd find it a most unpleasant sight. He was very decomposed, you know."

Penny was crestfallen. "I've seen plenty of bodies before," she wheedled, "I'm really not at all squeamish."

"No, I'm sorry."

"All right then, can you give me the autopsy findings?"

"Yes, that I can. Would you like the details technical or straight?"

"Straight," said Penny, who was a stout believer in simplicity.

"Oh, O.K. then. Male, Caucasian, about thirty-five years old, five-foot-seven, medium build but broad-shouldered, dark curly hair. Eyes gone so color not known. Killed by several blows on the head by an implement that had a sharp edge to it and was probably metal—in other words not a rock."

"Possibly a shovel or spade?" Penny queried, thinking of the excavation.

"Could be. The really odd feature is the mutilation of the face post-mortem; probably several days post-mortem."

"How did they figure that?"

"The face was badly mangled by repeated blows and earth was found impacted into some of the bony structures that remained, indicating that at least some degree of decomposition had started before it happened." He grimaced. "As I said, it's not very pleasant."

"But if he had been in the water all that time how was all that preserved?"

"Oh, he was in a burlap bag which protected at least parts of him, though it too had rotted."

"Has that been identified?"

"Yes, it was one of a bunch that came from a shed at the edge of the bog."

"The one by Zeb Grange's?"

"That I don't know."

"But the body was naked?"

"Yes, completely, and apparently bundled into the bag and shoved into the culvert either just before or just after the flooding of the bog. The pathologist can't pinpoint a day obviously."

"But sometime in September?"

"Late September, very early October. Normally speaking, the body would have been a lot *more* decomposed except for the freakish winter we had. The bogs froze solid in October and stayed that way almost to mid-February, so it slowed the decomposition down. We even managed to get some fingerprints off some of the fingers. Not that it did much good, I'm told. They sent them off to the FBI, but his prints are not on file there or in the Pentagon."

"How about his teeth?"

"Again, nothing much to go on. A good, strong set with no fillings and just one or two small cavities. Obviously hadn't been to a dentist in a very long time, if ever—a lot of tartar build-up, and the teeth were very uneven."

"In what way?"

"The left maxillary canine was markedly procluded, with a corresponding malformation of its opposing mandibular canine, which was also procluded and distorted—what in common terms would be called a 'wolf' canine in the upper jaw and a 'pig-tooth' sticking out to match it in the lower."

The hairs on the nape of Penny's neck rose. "Good Heavens! And dental patterns are so often hereditary, aren't they?" she murmured faintly.

"I believe so. Why?" He looked at her with curiosity.

"Just an idea. Would you do something for me?"

"That depends on what it is." For a second he was very much the proper mortician.

"Take the cephalic index on the head—or let me do it."

"Measure the skull? What do you hope to prove?"

"I'll just make a small bet that it is very roundheaded. Will you do it?"

"Oh, all right." He went out with a mystified look on his face and came back looking even more so. "You were right. Brachycephalic as all get out—an extreme round-head."

"In other words, taken together with the rest of his build, an extreme Alpine type," Penny murmured. "Ergo, he *could* be an Italian."

"Or half a dozen other nationalities," the young man interjected. "Isn't that sort of thing a bit old hat?"

"In general, yes, almost useless, but in this particular instance it might be significant," she said, but did not elaborate further. "Was there anything else interesting in the findings?"

The young man ran through the sheaf of papers in his hand: "His left wrist had been broken, probably some time during puberty, and what skin remained on the palms of the hands did indicate some calluses, as if he'd done rough work at some time. The nails, on the other hand, were fine, rather delicate and well cared-for. Not like, say, a mechanic's or a construction worker's or even a seaman's. That's rather curious too, come to think of it."

Penny sighed. "And he does not fit the description of any missing person locally or in New England?"

"Not that the police have discovered so far."

"And the inquest is when exactly?"

"Tomorrow at Barnstable County Court, 2 o'clock, I believe."

"And then you'll bury him, even if you still don't know who he is?"

"Yes, he'll be buried as a John Doe in the Masuit cemetery. Our storage facilities here are pretty limited, we're not like a big city where they have a regular morgue, but we can always get him up again if necessary. He's O.K. now, we embalmed what was left." This seemed to cheer him up considerably.

Feeling she had probably got all she was going to get out of Dave Baxter, Penny thanked him effusively and they parted. As she hurried back to the Langley cottage, Penny felt a mounting excitement about the anticipated luncheon with the Dimolas. Now she could hardly wait to test her burgeoning theory.

In this she was doomed to disappointment, for pinned to the door was a note from Ann to say the Dimola luncheon had had to be postponed—no reason given—and would Penny make it dinner with them tomorrow. "Hobson's choice," snarled Penny, and went grumpily off to finish her letter to Toby.

She was not left long in peace, however, for hearing noises in the lounge she went out to find Officer Birnie there with a rather worried-looking Ann in tow. "He wants us to go to Zeb's place to see if we can spot any other missing items," Ann explained. She sounded unenthusiastic but Penny jumped at the opportunity, though she knew perfectly well she could be of little or no help.

They were met at the house by the indignant mammoth cat, who had to be placated with food before they could proceed with their search. "If only you could talk," Penny mourned, as she watched him systematically demolishing a huge bowl of milk, "between us we could have this thing sewn up in a jiffy."

Ann checked the considerable Indian collection upstairs and averred to the best of her knowledge nothing was gone. Penny elected to go through the notes on the desk and Ernie Birnie applied himself to the file cabinet. Penny went diligently through the neat piles of "dig" notes, archaeological journals and offprints with which the desk was laden. She had little hope of finding anything significant but wanted to see what Zeb had been up to on the dig, for yet another idea had just struck her. She deftly separated his notes on the Indian cemetery and the grid plan of the site from the rest and, with a quick look to see that Birnie was not watching, slipped them into her sling bag for further study. A quick riffle through the rest of the papers brought to light just one anomalous scrap, a single leaf torn from a scratch pad on which Zeb had been doing some strange sums. It read: "1978–34 = 1944? Possible"; then "1944–5 1st plt. CE 3rd Div. RD PC? check. It. Camp. Imola?" It made no sense, but that too disappeared into her pocketbook. "Nothing here," she announced, and got up to join Ernie Birnie who was frowning at something, his lips pursed in a silent whistle. "What have you found?" she asked him.

"If it *had* been murder, one dandy little motive," he mumbled, too engrossed to realize he was talking to the enemy.

She squinted sideways at the paper in his hand and her own eyes widened. It was an insurance policy for $150,000, with a double-indemnity clause for accidental death. "Who is the beneficiary?" she whispered, and answered her own question, "Carson Grange, the nephew."

Birnie came to with a start and glared at her. He asked, "Not that it's any of your business, but did you find anything gone?"

"Nothing at all," she said sweetly, "and I think this is a complete waste of time since we don't know what he had to start with." Nonetheless he doggedly insisted they make an inspection of every room before admitting defeat. He ended up in the dining room, gazing in frustration at the faint mark in the dust. "TV here, typewriter, stereo, silver . . . all here except for that blasted photo," he fretted. "If it was a sneak thief, it sure was a strange one!"

Penny refused to join battle again. "Is there any late word on Zeb's condition?" she asked.

"No, condition stable but unchanged. The doctor says he could stay that way for days, months or years, no telling about it. They'll let us know the minute there's any change and we'll send someone over pronto."

"You mean he's unguarded?" Penny said in sudden alarm. "But what if another attempt on him is made?"

"Only unguarded in a manner of speaking." He gave her a savage grin. "We're not that stupid, you know, even if we can't spare a policeman to camp outside his door. *No one* gets in to see him, and no one had better try if they know what's good for them!" And on that triumphant note he took his leave.

They picked up Penny's young namesake and got back to Ann's cottage in exhausted silence. "I'll start supper," Ann said, and disappeared into the kitchen. "And I'll make us a drink," Penny volunteered, but they were almost immediately startled out of their domestic clatter by a pounding on the door. "I'll get it," Penny called, and Ann came wide-eyed to the door of the kitchen, wiping her hands on her apron.

Penny swung the door open to confront a young man in the gray uniform of a state trooper. Elation briefly surged in her; Detective Eldredge must have relented and sent this young man to fill her in on the murder after all. "Oh, you've come about the body in the bog?" she said brightly. "Do come in."

The young man took off his trooper's hat and stepped across the threshold, and as he turned his profile to the light a resemblance leaped out at Penny; she saw at the same instant that he was red with suppressed fury. "I most certainly have not come about the murder," the young man snapped, "I have come about Zebediah Grange, and I want to know what the devil you did to him, and what you were doing searching in his house!"

"I don't understand," Penny stammered, "I thought the local police were handling that. We were there with one of them. What business is it of the state police?"

"It's very much *my* business," the young man roared, "I'm Zeb's only close kin—I'm Carson Grange!"

CHAPTER 7

As Penny faced up to the angry young man she felt a sinking certainty that Zeb's eccentricity and single-mindedness was a hereditary trait in the Grange family. Patiently she explained Zeb's summons to her, showed him the two letters, introduced Ann—who hastily confirmed her story —explained their presence in the Grange house as the official summons of the Barnstable police, referred him to Officer Birnie as reference and generally tried to calm him down.

His initial anger gradually faded, but he remained truculent and suspicious, and things were definitely not progressing any too well when young Penny innocently entered on the scene and saved the day. Roused from her nap by the unaccustomed deep, booming voice in the house, she came toddling sleepily out to investigate, took one look at the tall young man and marched purposefully toward him, her arms raised. "Dada?" she asked hopefully.

It was as if someone had waved a magic wand over Carson Grange; his truculence disappeared in a flash and his weather-beaten, long-jawed face broke into a delighted grin, revealing white, even teeth. He squatted down and took the small hands in his large one. "Hi there, young lady, and who might you be?"

Ann went a bright pink. "Oh dear, I'm afraid she has a tendency to do that," she apologized, and a further introduction was made.

Carson was quite unfazed by this new development. In fact he appeared to have forgotten his initial hostility and, for that matter, the object of his visit. He settled cozily down in a chair with young Penny on his knee and accepted the offer of a drink from a relieved elder Penny. "Have a boy of my own about this age," he informed them. "Fascinating stage, isn't it?" The two women perched uneasily with their own drinks and gazed rather bemusedly

57

at the animated conversation that was developing between the rugged trooper and young Penny, who suddenly seemed to have an endless stream of information to impart.

The vision of the $150,000 insurance policy danced before Penny's eyes and she tried to imagine this young man cold-bloodedly striking his uncle down and arranging the accident scene. For all of his air of suppressed violence she found it difficult to do. But he did have a quick temper, that was very evident; a quarrel, a sudden blow, his uncle face down in the mud, turning him over and, in a sudden panic, fleeing—yes, that would be conceivable. But there was still that wretched whisky bottle which pointed to premeditation, and this she found hard to accept either.

It's an old saw that children always know people's natures better than adults, she thought, they scent danger like animals do, and so if that's a Golden Rule, he's as harmless as a newborn babe—I've never seen such instant empathy between a child and an adult. Moreover she could certainly use an ally; by the determined set of Carson's jaw, he looked as if he would make a formidable one. She decided to follow her instinct. When she could get a word in edgewise between the enraptured pair, she said, "Mr. Grange, I am deeply concerned about what has happened to your uncle, and since you are obviously equally concerned, I feel that I should explain my part in all this."

His face sobered and he again looked dangerous. "Yes, I would very much like to know about it and about you. The local police have been very tight-lipped about the case and I know virtually nothing."

Rapidly she sketched out her role in the affair, the letters from Zeb and her finding of him in the bog. "About that there is one very puzzling thing, something I hope you can enlighten me on. You must realize that I had not set eyes on your uncle for some thirty years up to last fall and I know virtually nothing about him, so I'm not asking this in a spirit of nosiness but merely as a vital bit of information —was your uncle an alcoholic or an ex-alcoholic?"

He frowned and hesitated before replying. "Up to two years ago when I moved to the Cape I had known very little of my uncle at all, but since that time I've seen him frequently and I can say without reservation ·that, during that period, he has never taken a single drink, nor has there been any alcohol in his house. Why?"

Penny told him and added, "And what I found more than a little strange was that the local police did not make a single mention of either the bottle or of the whisky odor on him—almost as if they knew he had a problem and were covering up. But they missed something—your uncle had not *drunk* any of the whisky. It was just made to seem so by his attacker."

"I see," he said slowly. "Well, in that case . . . yes, you're right. He told me that after his accident he was terribly despondent for a time and tried to drown himself in a bottle, but that Rinaldo pulled him out of it; sent him to a clinic in Vermont and then watched over him like a mother hen when he came out."

"The omnipresent Rinaldo," Penny murmured.

"Tell me, what kind of whisky was it?" Carson asked unexpectedly.

Penny tried to picture it. "Canadian Club," she said at last.

"Then whoever did it knew something of Zeb's former history but not enough." His tone was decisive. "You see I know for a fact that Zeb never drank anything but Scotch and one particular brand of Scotch at that—Johnny Walker. He told me so himself. So it *was* a plant."

"But I suppose with all the recent stress he was under since last fall he could have been tempted and he *could* have changed his taste," Penny demurred.

"Zeb change? Never! Anyway, I would never have let him baby-sit Bobby for an instant if I thought he had gone back to the bottle, and there was *never* any sign of it in the last six months."

"Baby-sit Bobby?" Penny looked at him in dumbfounded amazement at this new insight into Zeb's domestic activities.

Carson's jaw jutted a little further. "Yes, well when Bobby's regular baby-sitter couldn't look after him and I was on duty, Zeb often used to take him—they got on very well. I'm a single parent," he explained.

"Why so am I!" Ann exclaimed, breaking her rapt silence. They appraised one another for a critical moment as if doubting the other's capabilities as a parent.

"So that certainly seems to bring me right back to my

original view that Zeb was silenced before he could talk to me of this other affair and that a clumsy and ineffectual attempt was made to have it *look* like an accident," Penny said. "So we are back to the body in the bog, and here I could certainly use your help since you're with the state police."

He squirmed in his chair. "But I'm not actually involved in that; the South Yarmouth police are handling it. I work out of Bourne. Anyway, why are you so sure there is a connection?"

"I wish I were *sure,* but it's the only thing that makes any sense. Zeb specifically mentioned the Pergama affair in which I was recently involved and which was a question of murder and drugs. When he took me to the Indian graveyard he obviously was going to show me something in that grave. Whatever it was was gone, and this terrified him. Then comes the finding of the body this spring and his second summons to me. Ergo, I assume that *that's* what he expected to find and that somehow it is all tied in with the Dimola family, specifically Rinaldo, because of your uncle's evident and fanatical devotion to him."

"You think Rinaldo may have murdered someone?"

Penny threw up her hands in despair. "I just don't *know,* and until I meet the Dimolas I really can't say anything further. But you must know the officers on the case and could be of enormous help in passing on details of their findings to me and in trying to convince them there is a connection between the cases. I have tried and failed, but they might listen to you. There's still so much to find out. Will you be going to the inquest?"

"No, I'll be on duty, where, unfortunately, I must go now as well." He disentangled himself from young Penny's fond embrace and got up. "But I'll do what I can. I'm as anxious as you are to get to the bottom of this, Dr. Spring. I suggest we work together and pool information." He turned to Ann with an engaging smile. "Is it all right if I come around tomorrow? I could bring Bobby to play with Penny?"

"I'm afraid we're booked for then," Penny said hastily. They settled for early afternoon the day after and he took his leave over the protestations of the toddler. "I wonder what happened to his wife," Ann said thoughtfully, as she towed her howling offspring away.

The inquest was underway, the twelve good men and true, headed by a formidable-looking forewoman, installed in their box, the judge-coroner on his bench, and a very young-looking assistant D.A. questioning the witnesses. Penny found herself gazing at the open-mouthed gilt codfish dangling from the ceiling of the old county courtroom and feeling great empathy with its bewildered expression; she was feeling that way herself.

The evidence of the discovery of the body had been taken from the young Robert Dyke, who had gone a faint green again at the very recollection of his unexpected find and had hurriedly left the courtroom after his testimony. He was followed by a young man from the county pathologist's office, who went over the medical report, which contained all the same data Penny had already heard but to which the jury listened with pop-eyed attention. And he was duly followed by a middle-aged, quiet-looking man who turned out to be the foreman in charge of the Dimola Enterprises cranberry bogs. Penny sat up and took notice.

The foreman appeared to be nursing a faint grievance against Robert Dyke. "Trespassing he was," he said severely. "Those bogs are clearly posted; he had no right to be there."

"Luckily for the interests of justice he was," the assistant D.A. put in, "otherwise the body might not have been discovered so quickly. But kindly confine yourself to answering my questions, Mr. Jones. Now. When and why was that bog flooded?"

The foreman cogitated. "First week in October, and we flood them every year to protect the bushes from frost damage, same as always." He seemed positively aggrieved by the assistant D.A.'s ignorance.

The forewoman of the jury, who had become so interested in the proceedings that her massive bosom was now resting on the rail of the jury box, boomed unexpectedly, "Kind of early for the flooding, wasn't it, Bill? Some folks hadn't finished harvesting by then."

The young D.A. gave her an annoyed glance and the judge-coroner, starting out of a postprandial doze, rapped for order. "By whose orders were the bogs flooded that early?" the D.A. continued.

"Mr. Dimola's, Mr. Steven Dimola's." Penny's interest quickened. So it was not Alexander, Rinaldo's right hand in the main business, who was occupied with the bogs, but the scholarly Steven; she wondered why.

"And was this arrangement usual?"

"Nothing was usual just then. Mr. Rinaldo Dimola had just got sick. It was him normally gave us the orders, the bogs being a kind of hobby of his, though most of the time he left it to me."

"And did Mr. Steven Dimola give any reason for this early flooding?"

Frowning, Jones pondered again and answered, "Far as I can recollect I did say it seemed a mite on the early side to me, then he said the meteorological"—he boggled over the word—"forecast was for a hard early freeze, and we'd better be prepared. He was right too. I never did see such a winter in all my years on the Cape." There was a sympathetic groan from the jury. "That bog froze in the second week of October and stayed froze till February."

"So it would have been impossible for the body to have been put in the bog during that whole period?"

"Not unless they chipped through the ice, which don't seem likely to me," Jones agreed.

"And the draining?"

"We had that warm spell the third week of February and I run most of it off then."

"On Mr. Steven Dimola's orders?"

"No, on my own. Wanted to see what damage had been done to the bushes—not bad as it turned out."

The assistant D.A. turned to the jury. "I should point out from the medical evidence that the body was too decomposed to have been put in the bog that late, so you may assume that it was placed in the bog either just before or just after the flooding of the bog in the first week of October." Then to Jones: "Now, could you tell us something about the inspection of the bogs. In other words, had it not been for Mr. Dyke's keen observation which led to the fortuitous find, how long would it have been before your inspection of the water depth in the drainage ditches revealed the body?"

The witness looked sullen. "Can't say for certain. We get a build-up of weed from time to time that has to be cleared out, but unless it gets real bad or we have a lot of rain . . . well, bogs take care of themselves mostly, till harvest. Might have been found then or, seeing as how it was stashed away in that there railway culvert, might not. Might never have been found."

"I see. Well, Mr. Jones, you may step down."

He was replaced on the stand by Detective Barnabas Eldredge of the state police, who narrated his part in the case and the so-far futile attempts to identify the body in the clipped flat accent of the native Cape Codder. He was a small, wiry, sandy-haired man, with a deceptively mild face which many people had, to their cost, been taken in by; Barnabas Eldredge was a lot tougher than he looked. The D.A. did not seem to be interested in probing much further, but the detective was not to escape that easily. He was about to step down when the forewoman of the jury waved a large meaty arm above her head as if to order a charge of the Valkyries. "I should like to ask a question," she boomed. The D.A. looked pained but the judge-coroner nodded. "You say you still have no idea who the man is, yet I've heard tell you are planning to bury him. Is that correct?"

"We held off as long as we could, but soon as the inquest is over he'll be buried as a John Doe, first thing tomorrow," Eldredge snapped.

The forewoman bridled. "No need to take that testy tone with me, Barney Eldredge. He's being buried then at the taxpayers' expense, so I've a right to ask. Seems to me there's a sight more you could do about finding out who he is before planting him out of our pockets. You know he's not a Cape man."

"I don't *know* that." Eldridge glared at her.

"No one missing from round here," she said firmly, and there was a murmur of support from her fellow jurors. "Seems to me you ought to send him up to Boston and let them handle it if it's beyond *you*, or do a sight more enquiring around here. How about the Dimolas? Have you questioned them? He was found on their land. Why don't they bury him? They can afford it." Penny felt an almost electric wave of hostility sweep through the courtroom as

Eldredge rapped out, "That's official business and none of yours."

"It is too my business as a Cape Cod resident and a taxpayer," she roared. "Pussyfooting, that's what you've been doing, Barnabas Eldredge. We don't want another Chappaquiddick—once was quite enough!"

A mild commotion erupted with everyone talking at once and the judge-coroner banging his gavel, trying to regain control. The incident both amused and shocked Penny a little, giving her a brief glimpse of an undercurrent of raw emotion and hostility that lay beneath the placid surface of the Cape. No one loves a rich relation, she thought to herself, and that seems particularly true around here. She felt a twinge of sympathy for the absent and unknown Dimolas —but were they absent? She took a quick look around the courtroom, which had more spectators than usual because of the interest in the case. A movement at the back caught her eye, and she saw a short, dark-haired girl slip quietly out of the double doors under cover of the now subsiding commotion. There was nothing remarkable about her, save perhaps for the fact she was wearing tinted glasses on a gloomy day, but was she one of them? Could be, Penny concluded.

Order had been restored and the jury charged to consider its findings. It filed out in rather mutinous silence and filed in again in what seemed a very short space of time. There was little doubt of what its verdict had to be: "Murder of a John Doe by person or persons unknown." But there was a characteristic rider, instigated no doubt by the unmollified forewoman: "That the police should bend every effort to uncover the identity of this John Doe and to discover his murderer."

Well, if they don't, I most certainly intend to, Penny thought, and for the first time felt a rise of confidence. If sympathetic vibes had anything to do with it, at least she knew the people of the Cape were with her all the way.

CHAPTER 8

What surprised Penny most about the Dimolas was their youth.

She had built up a mental picture of Rinaldo Dimola as the venerable patriarch of his clan, and of his family as mature and middle-aged. Now, looking down the long dinner table, she realized how absurd that notion had been. Rinaldo Dimola was only a handful of years older than herself; his elder son, Steven, now sitting at her right, a bare thirty years old; and the rest of the faces around the ornate table younger than that. The Dimolas were clearly clumped closely together in age. Alexander, now sitting on her left, could not be more than a year younger than Steven, and Maria, sitting next to the Dimola heir, only a couple of years younger than that. Ann Langley sat opposite to her and next to Alexander, and the three Dimola wives sat in a bunch at the bottom of the table: Annette at the head, impassive of face and poised, Inga to her right, Wanda to her left.

The Dimola men, Penny reflected, had remained true to the Italian preference for blondes, since all three wives were fair in varying shades: Inga with the typical ash-blonde hair of the Swede coiled around her large head in sleek braids; Wanda a platinum—which may have come out of a bottle—done in a short Hamell cut; and Annette with golden, silky hair done in a modified Farah Fawcett-Majors style that did not particularly suit her thin, Madonna-like face. But there was no doubt about it, they were all three extremely decorative.

Penny had been given the seat of honor at the head of the long table opposite Annette Dimola. She perched uneasily, practically engulfed by Rinaldo's high-backed Renaissance chair, feeling almost sacrilegious. Rinaldo was absent in body, but his spirit still brooded over the room, so that tones were muted in the sporadic conversations going on around the table.

The dinner was excellent, which for Penny, to whom good food was a true joy of life, proved a most tantalizing distraction from her chief task of observing. She kept up a polite chitchat with the slight and serious Steven and the hefty Alexander, who was indeed the image of his absent father, while she kept a watchful eye on the rest of the table.

Apart from the two men no one seemed to have much to say. Maria was completely silent, and stared in concentration at Penny with rather beady dark eyes. She was certain now that Maria was the girl she had seen at the inquest. Had she gone as a scout for the Dimolas or as an interested party, Penny wondered. Inga, in the seat beyond, said little because she was completely engrossed in her food, taking large helpings, polishing off her plate with a greedy zest, and then looking expectantly around for the next course. While Penny appreciated her warranted enthusiasm she thought it explained the meatiness of her large, full-bodied figure. If she goes on at that rate all the time, she'll be a blimp before she's forty, Penny thought.

By contrast Wanda Dimola was hardly eating a thing, toying with her plate and pushing it away after only a mouthful or two. She looked pale and strung out, and after the third course gave up all pretense of eating, lighting up cigarette after cigarette, which she would smoke for two or three jerky puffs and then mash out with a savage gesture of the slim, trembling hand. Annette Dimola was eating slowly and sparingly, as if unaware of what was before her. She occasionally would pass some remark to Inga or Ann but appeared to be ignoring Wanda. Bad blood there? or was Wanda a family problem? Something else to find out.

After a particularly succulent dessert of a Viennese nut torte with whipped cream heavily piled up, Annette leaned forward and addressed Penny directly. "Shall all of us take our coffee and liqueurs in the drawing room, Dr. Spring? We can talk more easily there."

They filed out haphazardly into the huge living room with its spectacular view of Massachusetts Bay. Even here, though most of the furniture was ultramodern and opulently comfortable, there were a few Italianate touches, such as a blue velvet seat-in-the-round, the like of which Penny had never seen anywhere but in Italian historical movies of the Risorgimento age, and a very ornate gaming table done in marquetry. It was evident that Rinaldo had to put his insignia everywhere, even on his son's living quarters.

They settled in a ring of chairs grouped around a very large teak Danish coffee table and looking out over the bay. Wanda had disappeared, and Ann went off with a murmured excuse that she had some letters to finish typing. After a few minutes Steven wandered out after her, a fact Penny noted with interest but which irked her, since she had been hoping for a little more intimate conversation with him than the dining table had afforded. Sipping her coffee, she was wondering how she was going to bring up her main burning interest when Alexander did it for her.

He put down his own cup and, clearing his throat, addressed her rather as if he were opening a board meeting. "Dr. Spring, we realize your deep concern over what has happened to Zebediah Grange and appreciate your determination to get to the bottom of this murderous attack. Let me say we feel exactly as you do. Zeb Grange is one of my father's oldest and dearest friends, someone we have known practically all our lives, so if there is anything any of us can do to assist you, you have only to say the word. Money, transportation, accommodations, whatever you need."

"That is very thoughtful of you, Mr. Dimola," Penny murmured, "but offhand I can't think of anything, except, perhaps, some information."

"Information?" His tone was suddenly wary.

"Yes. You see in a sense Zeb had already . . . well 'retained' I think is the proper word . . . my services on another aspect of this present situation, so my expenses have been taken care of. I have rented a car and, as you know, I am staying with Ann, who is an old student of mine and which seems to suit her so far."

"But with Ann going away I do feel you'd be more comfortable here," he cut in smoothly. "There is, as you see, lots of room, and you'd be spared time-consuming domestic worries."

"Ann going away?" Penny was startled, for Ann had made no mention of it.

"Oh, yes. Just for a couple of days. There is an important antique auction in New York she and Steven must attend. She always acts as Steven's buyer and bidder for obvious reasons." His tone was blandly arrogant. "So, in view of the fact that you'd be alone in the cottage, and I think that might be unwise, I do most strongly urge you to move up here."

Penny hesitated as she thought rapidly. She was being invited—almost summoned—into the lion's den. If it would give her an excellent chance of getting to know the Dimolas at first hand, on the other side of the coin, it would enable them to keep close tabs on her and her activities; and indeed—if one of them was a murderer—might be dangerous. However, she was making precious little headway in her present state—so "dare all, gain much," she concluded. "Well, thank you for the invitation, if it's really all right with you. I'm afraid I come and go rather a lot." She looked enquiringly at Annette, who had sat silent through the exchange.

"No trouble at all," Annette murmured in her low, melodious voice, "though I'm afraid we are not a very lively household, Dr. Spring, due to my husband's physical condition."

"I understand that, and I was very sorry to hear about his illness, but I believe Mr. Dimola is showing signs of improvement, is he not?"

A faint animation came into the impassive face. "Yes, there are signs that his speech may be returning—the doctor has great hopes . . ."

Alexander cut her off. "Er, you said 'information,' Dr. Spring. I must say that rather puzzles me. All of us were terribly shocked by what happened to Zeb Grange, but we know nothing about the attack other than what Ann has told us."

Again Penny hesitated. Shock tactics might be dangerous at this early stage, but she decided they were worth a try. "Oh, not information about that," she said, "but about the business Zeb was consulting me on—the reason he was attacked."

"What business was that?"

"Why, the murder, of course," she said blandly, "the body in the bog."

A cold silence congealed around her as they all stared at her; Inga's pale blue eyes were narrowed, Annette's hazel ones shrewdly appraising, Maria's veiled, Alexander's hard. "I'm afraid I don't understand," he said stiffly. "What possible connection could Zeb have had with that—and how could it possibly concern us?"

"I have every reason to believe he knew about the body as far back as last fall and that he was silenced because he knew more about it—probably the man's identity—than someone local cared to have revealed, someone who got wind of the fact he was about to reveal it to me. And as to how it concerns you, I am further convinced that the murdered man was in some way connected with your father or your father's business."

"But what makes you believe that?" Alexander exploded angrily.

"Because when I was summoned here last fall Zeb refused to tell me *at that time*. It must have been just after your father's stroke, and I don't think he felt he could reveal anything to me until he talked with your father."

"You were here last fall?" Alexander seemed stupefied by this news.

"Indeed I was." Penny decided to stretch the truth a little. "Just after Zeb had found the body, but by the time I got here it had been moved from its original hiding place." She decided to back-pedal a little. "It's a great misfortune that the two cases are being handled by two separate police forces, when they should be considering the two as one. But in some ways this may be an ultimate advantage. Zeb, I am certain, was protecting your father's interests, and *I* am interested in protecting Zeb's, so anything you can tell me will be of help. I hope you can see that. You can help me enormously by just clearing the ground for me. For instance, have any servants left or disappeared during that time?"

The tension seemed to ease a little. "Only one of the groundsmen, and he took a job in Osterville," Annette said.

"Were you expecting any visitors or businessmen here who did not show up when expected?"

Annette seemed about to say something but Alexander said abruptly, "None. We have done very little entertaining here in the last two years, and none at all since my father's stroke. And he kept all business conferences for Boston. This was where we came to relax, where we escaped from business." His tone was almost bitter.

"And were you all here when your father was stricken?"

"As a matter of fact we were. It was on a weekend, a Saturday, as I recall, in the morning."

"Could you tell me a little more about that?"

"Well, let's see. It was quite late in the morning. My father was in his study. Zeb had been up to see him earlier. The rest of us were mostly outside—playing tennis, I think—because it was a beautiful spell of Indian summer. Inga went in to see if he wanted to go sailing after lunch, it was such a beautiful day. She found him slumped over his desk, called the rescue squad, called us, then we all went off with him to the hospital. That was about it, wasn't it?" he appealed to Inga, who nodded nervously.

"He was taken to Cape Cod Hospital in Hyannis?"

"Yes. He stayed there . . . oh . . . two or three days. Then his own doctor from Boston decided he could be brought back here, since we had all the facilities and he felt the home atmosphere might bring him around quicker."

"And the date of his stroke?"

"September 29," Alexander said promptly.

"And I was here on the 8th of October," Penny murmured. "So somewhere around or between those dates a man came to Masuit and was murdered, his body buried, his body moved . . . A busy person the murderer was that week." She looked at them steadily, her mild hazel eyes suddenly hard. "Busy but unfortunate."

"Why do you say that?" His voice was subdued.

"Because it was ill luck that Zeb discovered the body in the first place, even worse that I happened to be around at the same time, and most unlucky of all that the body was rediscovered and Zeb called me in again. An ill-starred murderer."

"You surely don't believe in astrology, Dr. Spring?" Maria spoke for the first time, and her tone was faintly mocking.

"Such stuff and nonsense, all of it!" Inga snorted. Annette seemed to draw further into herself.

Penny returned to the attack. "Have you any idea what

precipitated your father's stroke. Any sudden worry or anxiety, any unusual pressure?"

Alexander shook his head. "None. In fact, quite the opposite. The few weeks before his stroke he seemed far more like his old self than he had been for, oh, about two years—as if he'd solved some problem that had been weighing on him and that all was well again."

"A business problem?"

He knitted his heavy brows. "Well, there are always some problems around in a business the size of ours, but nothing at all serious."

"Did your father have any great enemies? After all, he is a very powerful man."

For the first time Alexander laughed, revealing strong, white and even teeth. "Really, Dr. Spring, I think you've been seeing too many movies. The wicked head of a financial empire grinding the faces of the poor, etc., etc. No, my father is a man who makes friends, not enemies. His is not the kind of business acumen that flourishes on the misfortunes of others. Rivals he may have, enemies, no. And we have no trouble with the Syndicate or the Mafia, and I don't go around with a gun under my armpit to protect my father's back." He smiled at her indulgently and shook his head. "In fact multimillionaires don't lead half as exciting lives as people think they do, nor are they very different from anyone else. The Howard Hugheses are the exception, not the rule."

Maria threw back her head and laughed suddenly, and Penny felt a little thrill of discovery—her teeth were strong, white and even too, but one was missing; her left incisor had been removed, and Penny could see the thin flash of gold on the small bridge to the inserted false tooth. "You shouldn't be in such a hurry to take father off the hook," she said to her brother. "The next thing you know Dr. Spring will be having the rest of us under her detecting glass. So to save you time, I don't have any enemies either that I'd want to murder and plant in a bog, no ex-husbands, no spurned lovers, no one."

"But you were interested enough in the man in the bog to go to the inquest today," Penny murmured.

There was another dead silence as the family looked at Maria with accusing reproach. "Well, yes, I did go," she said with a toss of her black hair and a shade defiantly. "I wanted to see what was going on; I'm as curious about things as you are."

"And how about your husband?" Penny turned to Inga. "This is your home. Was he expecting anyone who never came? Does he have any enemies?"

It was strange to see the large woman shrink back at this, her eyes becoming wide and frightened. "Why no," she stammered, "of course not!" Then her color mounted and her eyes began to flash. "Steven have enemies? No, that is not true! Everybody *loves* him. It is unpardonable what you say. Why do you accuse him?"

"I accuse no one . . ." Penny began, when she was interrupted.

"Someone accusing me of what . . . ?" Steven and Ann had come quietly back into the room. He advanced toward her with a slight smile, and this time she felt a real thrill of triumph. Unlike his brother's and sister's, Steven's teeth were not even—smaller than his father's but, nevertheless sticking out and dominating the mouth, was a wolf canine that gave his smile the same slightly sinister cast.

Penny got up. "I'm afraid your wife misunderstood me, Mr. Dimola, and I really feel I have inflicted myself on you all for far too long." She went over to her hostess. "Thank you for a very delightful dinner and a most informative evening, Mrs. Dimola. Are you sure in the light of all this you want me underfoot? I can make other arrangements if you would rather."

Annette took her proffered hand in her own cool one. "Believe me, Dr. Spring," she murmured softly, "I shall look forward to having you here, and I think it will be a very good thing—for all our sakes." And there was a wealth of meaning in her hazel eyes.

CHAPTER 9

Carson Grange moved like a shadow through the silent house. Room after room was subjected to the same meticulous search, drawer by drawer, closet by closet. The orange cat followed him with majestic interest, settling and watching with impassive amber eyes the large hands removing and replacing with impeccable neatness, so that all was as before. Beads of perspiration started out on the frowning brow as the search went on. Finally he stopped, looking around him in baffled puzzlement, then crossed to his uncle's desk again and opened the middle drawer which he had already searched; he slid it out and peered into the cavity behind. A small sigh of satisfaction escaped him and his groping hand withdrew a small packet of letters. Grim-faced, he read rapidly through them. "So he did keep them," he muttered through his teeth, "so they did mean something to him. Damn her, damn her to bloody hell . . . !"

Dark head and fair head were close together as the New York shuttle zoomed toward its destination. "I'm frightened, Steven. What if she finds out?"

"Finding out and proving are two different matters—you must not worry so."

"But she's clever and I've always been terrible at hiding things."

"I would say you hide things admirably." There was an ironic edge to his voice.

"You don't blame me then?"

"Blame you! Why of course not. What else could you have done in the circumstances? It should be easier now. Alexander might be a pain in some ways, but I have a lot of confidence in him. He'll take care of it—you'll see!"

"Do you really think so? Oh, how I wish it were all over."

73

"It will be. In the meantime all we can do is hang on. And wait. That's what we are both good at, isn't it? Waiting."

"You can go now, Pina, I'll stay with him for a while." Maria waited for the door to close, then crossed to the window and threw back the curtains; sleet tapped with icy fingers against the wide windows that looked over a gray, roiling sea, but inside the room it was hot and close, and she sighed as if short of breath. She walked over to the bed and looked at the burly figure propped up in the hospital bed, his eyes closed. She took the inert hand that was lying outside the covers and gave it a little squeeze. "It's me, Poppa, Maria."

The dark eyes so like her own slowly opened. "They're all busy now so we can have some time together. They always want to keep you in the dark about what's going on, but you don't want that, do you, Poppa? You like it when I tell you things?"

The heavy lids blinked twice for "yes." Maria gave a little sigh. "How bored you must be lying there, but it may not be for much longer, caro. I went to the inquest yesterday, in spite of them. Do you want me to tell you about it? You'd like that, wouldn't you?"

The lids blinked again and Maria settled on the edge of the bed, still holding the large hand in her two small ones. She began to talk rapidly, bringing the scene in the courtroom to vivid life; the witnesses, the jurors, the testimony. Becoming entranced in her own storytelling, she droned on almost unaware of the dark eyes fixed on her. Her animation increased as she reached the climax of her narrative: the commotion in the courtroom, the judge-coroner pounding ineffectually away for order. "Oh, it was so *funny*, Poppa, you should have . . ." Her words died away as she looked into his face, and she gave a little moan. "Oh, Poppa, Poppa, no! What did I say? Don't cry, oh, please don't cry!"

Annette Dimola looked with faint irritation at her stepdaughter-in-law. Although Inga was her senior by at least a couple of years she felt years older than the sullen

Valkyrie before her. "I don't see why you are so worried, Inga," she said, with as much patience as she could muster.

"I always worry when my Steven travels, always, until he has phoned he has arrived safely. One hears such terrible things. And when we are apart I worry about him anyway."

"But plane is a lot safer than car travel," Annette pointed out. It was an oft-repeated formula. Privately she wondered how Steven could bear this constant motherly hovering, the overwhelming possessiveness of his blonde bride, but she had long since concluded that secretly he must enjoy it. "Anyway if you are so worried, there is no reason why you couldn't have gone with him," she added.

"And then who would look after Poppa?" Inga demanded truculently. "I, I only, know what I am doing. What if he got worse when I was away? The rest of you are amateurs."

Annette heaved another inward sigh. She was not at all sure she had been wise in dismissing the trained nurses. She had let herself be persuaded by Inga and ever since had been subjected to this tyranny of professionalism. With all Inga's boasted-about training, Rinaldo was not coming to as quickly as Annette had hoped or the doctors had expected. Maybe I was wrong, she thought uneasily.

"And that woman who is here now—the one that said those bad things about Steven last night," Inga worried on, "who is she? Why must she be here? It is not good that she is here. What if she finds out about Wanda?"

"Yes, Wanda is a problem," Annette agreed, "but one I think we can safely leave to Alexander . . ."

"I've got to go to Boston today."

"*Again?* Then take me with you."

"Oh, for heaven's sake, Wanda! In this weather? I wouldn't go if I didn't have to."

"And you'll be gone overnight, I suppose?"

"And what's that supposed to mean?"

"You know damn well what I mean."

"Honestly, I don't know what's got into you. You never used to be like this. You're so strung out we can't seem to say a civil word to one another anymore. For the thousandth time, what's *bugging* you?"

"Oh, *everything*. This damn mausoleum, your father

lying up there like a zombie, your beloved family. I can't take it anymore. Why can't I go back home to Wellesley? There's nothing I can do here, and I never get to see you anyway, you're so damn *occupied*."

Alexander Dimola sighed wearily. "We've been over this same ground so many times. You know you can't stay in Wellesley by yourself, it's too dangerous. I *have* to stay here till we know which way it's going with father and till this latest mess is cleared up. Believe me, I'm sorry we can't have more time together, but I thought you'd at least understand that I'm carrying a double load just now and I have to keep an eye for and on Steven. If you're sick, as you keep saying, for God's sake see a doctor and stop pumping yourself full of this home remedy crap. Wanda, I'm almost at my wit's end—don't push me!"

"All right, all right!" She came very close to him, the beautiful face infinitely appealing, the exotic scent she wore reaching out to his senses. "I'll go and see a doctor. Take me to Boston and I'll go and see a doctor. Only *get me out of here*, or I swear I'll do something desperate!"

His shoulders slumped. "Very well," he said in a dull voice, "you win!"

Penny was looking out at her own gray seascape from the large window of her guest bedroom. She was still a little bemused by the opulence of her surroundings and the exotic quality of the house, which was so alien to its setting. It stood on the seaward tip of a small isthmus formed by an inlet of the bay on one side and salt marsh on the other. At the narrowest part of the isthmus a high steel fence of ornamental spikes closed in the house from the rest of the estate. In the middle of the fence was an equally substantial wrought iron gate operated by an electric eye from the house; that, and several guard dogs she had seen flitting like dark shadows around the grounds, appeared to be the Dimolas' only security measures. She had seen no security guards, no mention had been made of a bodyguard—all of which seemed to support Alexander's statement of the night before that his father was not fearful of retribution from enemies. Indeed, considering the violent climate of the times, the Dimolas seemed almost nonchalant about their personal security.

The house itself reflected the same thing. Approaching from the landward side it was formidable and alien: an improbable concoction of stone and stucco looking for all the world like a fortified medieval Tuscan farmhouse of gargantuan proportions. But on the seaward side it was mostly windows: huge acreages of sliding glass that made it almost part of the sea and sand and filled it with their dancing light. It must cost a fortune to heat, she was thinking practically, when the door opened quietly and Annette came in. "I just wanted to see if you have everything you want, Dr. Spring, or if there is anything I can do for you."

"Everything is just fine, Mrs. Dimola. But there is something you can do for me. Won't you come in and sit down for a while?"

They settled in two easy chairs grouped around a small table at the window, and Annette looked enquiringly at Penny, who said, without preamble, "The most valuable thing you can do for me at the moment is to talk. Tell me about your husband, for I am convinced that in him lies the key to all this."

Annette sketched a helpless little gesture in the air. "I wouldn't know where to begin. What is it you want to know?"

"Anything, everything. Say whatever is meaningful to *you* about him."

Animation crept into the impassive face. "To me he is the most remarkable man in the whole world. He is so *involved* with life. Not in a materialistic way as you might think from his financial success, but in a responsible way: integrity, courage, devotion to friends and his family which almost goes beyond the bounds of reason—all of this is Rinaldo and so much, much more . . ." She broke off and shook her head vexedly. "Oh, I'm afraid this isn't any good . . . how can I make you see? Well, just to give you one instance: the accident that crippled Zeb—a runaway bulldozer that started a gravel slide. I expect you know about that. My father, who was an architect for Rinaldo, was killed in the same accident. Rinaldo managed to pull Zeb free, and when they got to him he was also trying like a madman to lift the bulldozer off my father by brute strength. But it didn't end there—oh my, no! Not only did he take care of all the material needs of Zeb and my mother

but he went much further than that. To me he was like a
devoted father . . ." Penny wondered if she realized how
revealing that statement was as she rushed on. "No matter
how busy he was he always had time to come to school
plays and things like that—oh, anything that was important
to me as a child. And when my mother died when I was in
my first year of college, and I was so broken up—we were
always a terribly close family—he had me come to live with
his family on all the vacations. When his first wife died not
too long after my mother, I could hardly believe my good
fortune when he asked me to marry him, because by that
time I would have gone through hell and high water for
him . . ." She stopped and gazed almost with defiance at
Penny.

"In his business there must be a lot of industrial acci-
dents," Penny said mildly. "Is he that concerned about all
of them?"

"Certainly—if the family is involved," Annette said
hotly, then bit her lip, as if she had said too much.

"I don't understand. How was the family involved in,
say, Zeb's accident?"

Annette looked away from her out over the gray seascape. "The boys were at the site that day, and one of the
workmen said he'd seen them playing around the bulldozer;
one of them might have accidentally started it."

"I see. Any idea which?" Penny asked. Annette shook her
head and continued to gaze out the window. Penny looked
at her thoughtfully. A close family and her father dead,
possibly at the hands of a Dimola—cause for a deep-seated
grudge, perhaps even a subconscious one, against the Dimolas? Perhaps even a grudge against Zeb for being alive
while her father was dead? She wondered if Annette was
really as impassive and collected as she seemed. A glance at
her watch told her she had not much time left before her
rendezvous with Carson Grange at the cottage, so she
hurried on to the next objective. "I understand your husband
changed in himself and in his mode of life a couple of
years ago. Can you clarify that a bit for me. Was there a
definite starting point for this change or did it come on
slowly?"

Annette took a minute before answering. "Yes, I think
there was a starting point. It was when Steven had got his

father all fired up about the family history and genealogy. We all went to Italy that summer. I remember Rinaldo was as enthusiastic as a small boy. He had served in Italy during the war and had stayed in the place that Steven had discovered was the original home of the family; it's in the north, I believe. He and Steven and Inga went off. I stayed in Rome with Maria to do some shopping and sight-seeing. I blame myself for that now, but World War II was before I was even born, so I really was not interested in seeing old battlefields and so on. Steven and Inga came back without him and said he had decided to stay on for a few days looking around Imola. They went off again and Alexander and Wanda came back about the same time . . ."

"They were on the trip too?" Penny interjected.

"Yes, but not with us. They had gone off to visit some of Wanda's relatives." Seeing the surprise on Penny's face, Annette smiled faintly. "Yes, Wanda is a second-generation Italian-American. She doesn't look it, does she? Anyway, when Rinaldo got back, well, he was all closed in on himself. He rushed us back home and from that time on seemed totally uninterested in the family history."

"Did he say anything? Give you any indication of why this was so?"

Annette shook her head. "No, I felt that revisiting the old places had stirred up unpleasant memories—Rinaldo had had a very hard time in the war. He was wounded and captured and they treated him very badly. I blamed myself very much for not going with him and I tried to get him to talk about it, but he never would."

Penny gave another hasty glance at her watch. "One last thing before I have to go. Do you think I could see your husband's study? Ann told me it is very remarkable."

Annette looked surprised. "Why of course. Please feel free to wander about the house as you please. But I'll take you there now."

It was just as Ann had described it. Across the threshold Penny had stepped back into the Renaissance. It was a library that would have graced a ducal palace: the dark paneling, the tapestry hangings, even an ancient heavy globe standing by the great black carved desk and its matching chair. An oil painting of a somber-faced Rinaldo was the only modern thing in the room—or, at least that was

Penny's first impression. Then she noticed a framed photo-graph on the window wall and crossed over for a closer look. It showed a stern-faced young Rinaldo with a group of soldiers, leaning against a half-track truck; behind there were cypresses and a typical Italian "torre" half obscured by the trees. Leaning closer she could make out the faint inscription—"Colle d'Imola. June 1944."

"That was my husband's platoon," Annette's voice came from behind her. "They are all dead now but Rinaldo."

CHAPTER 10

It had been on the tip of Penny's tongue to ask Annette for a copy of the picture, but she had thought better of it. There was another source she could try before showing her hand to the Dimola family. Like it or not, Toby would have to come in on this, she thought, as she hurried off to keep her appointment with Carson Grange. Toby was Johnny-on-the-spot and it would not hurt him to do a bit of detecting on her behalf; in fact it would serve him right for being so bloody-minded about coming with her.

She arrived late to find Carson pacing up and down before the closed cottage like a hungry cougar. "Where is everybody?" he asked querulously. "I was just about to give you all up as a bad job."

"Ann's had to go off on business, so I've moved up to the main house," Penny explained. "Sorry to be late."

"And where's little Penelope?" Carson went on, nursing his grievance. "Don't say she's carted the poor kid off too."

"No. She's staying in Masuit with the woman who baby-sits her normally."

His face fell. "So I won't see her."

"Not this time around, I'm afraid." She looked at him with interest. "You're very fond of children, aren't you?"

"They're a damn sight more interesting than adults," he agreed grumpily. "So what now?"

"Well, two main things. Could we first go to your uncle's house? I'm very keen to see if he has any photograph albums of the Dimola family. There's one particular one I'm after and I'd like to borrow it."

"He's got photos all right," Carson said, "but if you're looking for a duplicate of the one that's been stolen you're out of luck. I thought of that already and went through them yesterday."

"No, not that one, an earlier one," she said, but did not elaborate.

They went off to the lonely house and picked up the inevitable accompaniment of the orange cat. Carson watched her with curiosity as she hastily riffled through the pages of the neat albums, finally coming on the one she sought with a little squeak of satisfaction. "Hmm," he said, and looked at it critically. "World War II, before my uncle even knew Dimola. What's important about that?"

"Zeb was never in the army, was he?" Penny asked.

"No, just a bit too young for that war and by Korea he was too valuable home here."

"Were you in the forces?"

He scowled at her. "Yes, I was in the Vietnam fiasco—why?"

"I just thought you might be able to decipher these doodles I found of your uncle's—he must have made them quite recently and some of it looks like army gobbledy-gook." She produced the scrap of paper, which he studied with morose interest.

"Well, 'RD' is presumably Rinaldo Dimola, '1st plt. 3 CE 3rd Div.' could be first platoon, third division of the Corps of Engineers—which would make sense since he *is* an engineer. The 'PC' could be a person's initials . . ."

"Or prison camp," said Penny with sudden enlighten-ment. "He was a prisoner."

"Oh, I didn't know that! So I suppose the 'It. Camp.' could be an Italian camp, perhaps at the place he mentions, Imola."

"Or Italian campaign *at* Imola," Penny mused. "Anyway, that's why I want the photo. I have a friend out in Italy just now and I want him to do some checking for me. I wonder if there's another photo of Dimola smiling . . ." She hastily flipped through the album again, but all the photos of Rinaldo were either stern or solemn of face. "Oh, well, this will have to do," she said with a sigh, "at least these give me an inkling of why the big photo was stolen."

"Why?" His tone was nettled.

"Because he *was* smiling," Penny said to complete his mystification. "Now we can go on to the second thing I had in mind—you're being a great help," she comforted. "I'd like to go over to the Indian site and have you bear witness to whatever I find in that grave."

"You know," Carson said in a carefully controlled voice, "I'm really beginning to have serious doubts about you. *Are you crazy?* You've already told me Zeb dug it up and found nothing. Why the hell do it again?"

"Because Zeb was in such a hurry that day, expecting to find the body, that he may have overlooked something small *from* the body—a button, some hairs, something, *anything*, to *prove* the body was there, something to prove my theory right and that the local police can't ignore."

"Oh, O.K., at least there's some sense to that," he huffed.

He fetched digging tools, to which Penny added a sieve, and they set off in his car. Penny was about to give him directions when she noted with interest that he didn't need any; he was heading for the site like a homing pigeon. "So you know where it is," she said casually.

"Sure, Bobby and I often used to give Zeb a hand with it," he replied, bumping off down the narrow, overgrown track. "Kind of interesting so long as you don't let it get to you."

Weeds were starting to grow on the filled-in trenches but the outlines of the site were still clearly visible, and after a brief consultation of the site plan Penny led the way up the slope of the hill to the line of graves. "This is it," she said, and seized a shovel. The sleet had stopped, but it was still very cold.

"Here, why don't you let me do that," Carson volunteered. "It beats freezing."

"Oh, fine!" she accepted with gracious alacrity. "You dig and I'll sieve until we get down to the burial, then I'd better take over."

They set to work in silence, though Carson kept a careful eye on her as she sieved the spadefuls of loose earth, as if doubting her capabilities. Nothing rewarded their efforts until he was about two feet down, when he suddenly said, "What's that? I caught a flash of something as I dumped that last spadeful."

She pawed through the earth and came up with a muddy orange capsule. "Oh, it's nothing," she said airily, "some kind of cold capsule or something—probably dropped out of Zeb's pocket."

"Let me see it." There was a curious note in his voice.

She handed it over and he cleaned it off and then, very

carefully, twisted it open and took out and tasted a little of the powder inside with his tongue before screwing it back together again. "That's no cold capsule," he said in the same odd voice.

"What is it then?"

He cocked a strong eyebrow at her. "I can't be one hundred per cent sure until the lab tests it, but I think it's Speed." She looked blank. "It's an 'upper,' " he explained patiently, "a *drug*."

"Oh, *no!*" she moaned in dismay. "First murder, now drugs again! I must be hexed or John Everett is a prophet."

"Well, one thing I'm sure about," he said as he resumed digging, "it didn't come out of Zeb's pocket. That's a young person's turn-on, not his kind of scene at all."

Nothing further rewarded his efforts, and in a while he rested on his spade and said, "I think I'm getting near the bottom, I can see a pot."

"All right. I think you'd better let me take over now." Penny slid into the trench and was engulfed by it. Carson knelt on the edge peering down as she carefully cleared the Indian skeleton with whisk broom and trowel. "I wish Toby were here, he's the expert on this kind of thing," she said presently, as the outlines of the crushed skeleton became defined. "It's not that I don't know what I'm doing, but it's been so long since I did this I'm terrified of missing something. I'm an anthropologist not an archaeologist; people, not pots, are my forte. And even as a student my archaeological technique was nothing to write home about." Carson merely grunted but continued to watch intently. "You know," she went on, "I've been mulling over the sequence of events here and I'd like to try them out on you to see if you can spot any flaws in my thinking. Zeb saw this grave was disturbed, dug into it, and found the body. I don't think he knew who it was but he recognized a likeness— either of someone linked to Rinaldo or someone who *looked* like Rinaldo. He was in a fine old quandary because Rinaldo had already been stricken with the stroke so he couldn't consult him. Hearing about me being over here he called me in. *But* the murderer somehow got wind of this and the fact he had found the body, moved it, and also took steps to make sure that in the unlikely event it was found again no one else would recognize it. Hence the stripping of the body and the mutilation of the face. Yet the murderer then made no move against Zeb, which clearly indicates to me that it is someone who knows him well; well enough to know that as long as the body is tied in to Rinaldo, Zeb will keep quiet. Even when the body is found again, he still makes no move against him——"

"Why do you say 'he'?" Carson interjected. "Why not she? Neither the method of the murder nor the attack on Zeb would have taken any great strength. It could have been done by a woman."

"I was just speaking generally," Penny said mildly. "Naturally I haven't ruled out a woman, but it's so clumsy to go on saying 'he or she.' Anyway, to go on. The murderer *only* makes a move when he knows I'm on my way here again. Which indicates to me that Zeb in that intervening time may have found out who it was, may actually have tackled him about it, and was silenced before he could 'tell all' to me as he had indicated in his letter. The would-be murderer had an unlucky break in that his attempt did not succeed, but a lucky one when the cases were put in the hands of two separate police forces. He'll be sweating blood if Zeb shows any signs of coming out of his coma, but so far this is not the case, though luckily Officer Birnie has enough sense to see he is well guarded."

Carson Grange moved restlessly, sending a cascade of stones and earth down on Penny. "Which seems to leave you in a highly vulnerable position, I'd say."

"No, not really, not while I'm groping in the dark as I still am. The murderer knows Zeb didn't tell me anything, or I'd have already done something about it. He also knows that if he attacked me it would be a dead giveaway that the two cases were one and then he'd have two police forces on his neck. So, for the moment, I don't think I'm in the slightest danger—aah!" She suddenly pounced on something near the midriff of the skeleton and began to clean off the clinging sandy mud, then held the object up triumphantly to Carson.

"What is it?" With a frown he took the crooked red plastic object.

"Well, I can't be sure, but to me it looks remarkably like the bottom half of a 'cornu,' you know, those fertility charms made in the shape of a goat's horn. You find them all over the Mediterranean area, but particularly in *Italy,* mark you!"

"You also find them here," he pointed out. "Half the kids in America wear something along this line round their necks: ankhs, crosses, pukka beads or these things."

"I've seen them in metal over here, but never as big as this or in plastic. I have a duplicate of this from Italy on a key ring back home in Oxford, and I'm willing to bet that's exactly what this came off of—they're very flimsy, mine's always falling off. Anyway, one thing I *am* sure of, it's recent in the grave and certainly is no Indian artifact!"

"It's not very much," he growled as she burrowed feverishly on. The sleet had started again, which didn't help, and after a few minutes of silence he went on, "How much longer are you going to be? I'm freezing up here."

Penny eased her cramped limbs and stood up. "I guess I've done about all I can; this sleet is turning everything into a mud puddle. Let's take what we have to the police and fill this in again. If we can get them interested I'll have another go at it." She crawled out and helped him shovel enough back to cover the remains, then shivered her way back to the car. There they had a brisk argument as to which police they should take their finds to, which warmed them both up and which Penny won. "It only makes sense to take it to the Barnstable people in view of my previous statement to them," she said. "This backs it up, and they'll have to start taking things seriously. Then, when we've done that, you can brief your people and get them in on it too."

Disregarding the fact they were both mud-covered and wetly bedraggled, they drove into Hyannis and to the police station on North Street, where their decrepit state raised the eyebrows of the policeman on the desk. With some difficulty they managed to convince him they had urgent business with Detective Thompson, and when they were ushered into his office found him in conference with a glum-faced Officer Birnie. The latter's eyes narrowed suspiciously as Penny introduced Carson Grange, but he said nothing as Thompson waved them to seats and asked in an improbable New York accent what could he do for them or what was on their minds.

Penny launched enthusiastically into her recital, to which he listened, eyes downcast, face expressionless, and twiddling a pencil between meaty fingers. Only when she got to the finding of the capsule did he look up, and after Carson had handed it over with some reluctance, went through the same performance of unscrewing it, tasting it, and pronouncing that it was indeed Speed. He looked across at Birnie and smirked. "Another nail in his coffin, I'd say. Nice bit of corroborative evidence with the rest of what we've got."

Birnie looked even gloomier, and Penny, who had been halted in mid-flow of her recital and whose mind was still firmly fixed on the body, said, "You mean you've found out his identity? You think this may be linked with him too?"

Thompson looked blandly at her. "Oh, you're still harping on that, are you? Well, I don't know anything about all that, nor do I know exactly what you think you're playing at, Dr. Spring. But I should point out that, although you seem to think otherwise, we are policemen and we *do* know our business. You can stop worrying about finding out who attacked Zeb Grange. You see, we found him and we arrested him this morning. We got our man!"

CHAPTER II

"I don't believe it, I'm sure you've got the wrong man. It just isn't *right,* he doesn't fit in at all!" Penny was so upset that she was comforting herself with a hamburger and french fries in the Hyannis Howard Johnson's. Across from her in the dark blue booth Carson Grange and Officer Birnie made an ill-assorted couple, sitting shoulder to shoulder and despondently sipping coffee; of the two Ernie Birnie, for all his official success, was looking the gloomier.

"I'm no happier about this than you are," he sighed. "I've known that kid since grade school; he and my boy have been friends for years. But there's a case against him all right, particularly now with the stuff you brought in— motive, means, opportunity." He ticked them off on meaty fingers. "He and Zeb Grange have been feuding over that damn Indian site all along, and he's been heard to threaten Grange with violence. We have a witness who saw him running away from the bog that day. Then there's this drug business. He's been in trouble over marijuana before, and we've had our eye on him for some time, thinking he might be involved with pushing pills to the local kids. On top of that is the physical evidence—bog mud and blood on that old pair of sneakers we found in his house, and the key to the padlock on the cranberry barn, which he may have lifted from Zeb. We think from signs in the barn he must have been using it as a drop point for someone on the estate; maybe he used the Indian site as well. No, it looks like Eagle Smith all right."

"But just because he was on the bog that day needn't mean anything," Penny protested. "What does he say about it?"

"Not a damn thing, the young fool. He's hell-bent on being the impassive Indian martyr—a latter-day Cochise suffering for his people. Just sits and smiles and won't say a word, which does not help him one damn bit."

"But can you honestly see him deliberately clubbing Zeb down and leaving him to die in the mud? Does he strike you as capable of that?"

Birnie looked gloomier than ever. "I know he's a king-size pain in the a—neck, and I can well believe he might be mixed up in popping and peddling pills, but, no, I wouldn't have thought him vicious. He's a big mouth, but for all his talk he has never been involved in any local violence. Still, who knows with kids these days . . ." he trailed off. Then, "Anyway what I think doesn't matter, Thompson is convinced of it and he's going to keep him in the slammer until the kid admits it or Grange comes around enough to tell us. The kid can't raise bail, he and his folks are dirt poor. What mainly worries me is what this is going to do to the community. There's been bad blood locally ever since the Mashpee land case. Now the Indians are going to say he's being railroaded *because* he's a militant Indian, and the rest are going to say that the Indians are getting dangerous and there'll be general hell to pay. Thompson, not being a local man, just doesn't appreciate that side of it."

"And I'm with the Indians," Penny said stoutly. "On the flimsy evidence you've got it seems to me he *is* being railroaded. Detective Thompson steadfastly refuses to believe this other evidence that links Zeb's attack with the bog murder. He simply disregarded our other find in the grave —wouldn't even listen!"

"You mean that red plastic doodad? I can't see that means anything myself. It could have been the kid's as well, if he was using the grave as a drop."

"An Indian with an Italian 'cornu'?" Penny said heatedly. "Out of the question. It would mean nothing to him. Besides, it was at the *bottom* of the grave. It strikes me you are overlooking one important thing, one thing that might explain the blood on Eagle Smith's sneakers and his hurry to leave the bog that day; *someone* was not about to let Zeb die, choked in the mud of that ditch, someone turned him over and then was scared off by my approach—remember, I heard that movement in the bushes—someone who, either because he had no legal business there or because he was known to be at odds with Zeb, was too scared to stay around. That someone could be Eagle Smith who, far from clobbering Zeb, may well have saved his life."

Birnie looked at her with narrowed eyes. "You may have something there," he admitted.

"Then why don't you ask him?" Penny urged.

"I doubt if he'd talk to me—he doesn't trust anyone in a uniform."

"Then what about letting me see him and talk to him?"

"Thompson would never go for it. Besides, why would Eagle talk to you either?"

"Because all through my career I've fought for Indian rights. I've fought for the Fox, the Pueblo, even for the Apaches," Penny said heatedly. "I happen to be one of the unpopular minority who think the Indians in this country have had a *very* raw deal, and who have tried to *do* something about it. Perhaps it's time for me to start fighting for the Wampanoags. If Eagle Smith knows anything at all about the rest of the Indian movements, he would at least have heard of me, so there must be *some* way to get to him and open him up. I'll just have to get him out. Maybe I can get the Dimolas to stand bail for him. In the meantime, Officer Birnie, may I make a pact with you? I know you think I'm an infernal nuisance, but I'm interested in the truth just as you are and I'm convinced I'm on the brink of a breakthrough on the bog murder, although I still have a lot to find out. I have sources closed to you and you have sources closed to me. If I keep you informed of what I find out, will you do the same for me?—particularly about Eagle Smith?"

"Sounds fair enough," he agreed cautiously, "but don't expect too much from me, and I still think you're barking up the wrong tree."

Later, as Carson drove her back to Masuit, she remarked, "I do hope he means what he said. Do you think he will help?"

"He might, particularly since he doesn't believe Eagle Smith is the culprit. He has a better suspect in mind."

"Oh? Who's that?"

"Me." Carson smiled grimly at her. "Birnie tends to be a bit elephantine in his approach. While you were arguing with Thompson, he asked me if I knew my uncle carried life insurance. As it happens I did. When I admitted this he came on a bit stronger. Did I know the beneficiary? I knew that too. It's a fairly new policy and $150,000 is a lot of money, especially for a cop who is trying to keep his son out of the hands of his blackmailing wife. You see my wife ran off with another man two years ago. At that time she wanted no part of Bobby any more than she wanted me. Now she and her boyfriend are hard up and she's trying to get money out of me, using Bobby's custody as a club—she knows the courts usually tend to favor the mother. There's a limit to what you can get out of a state cop's salary"—he grimaced—"but she even tried to put the arm on Zeb, telling him all sorts of lies about me. Not that he had much either, but with that insurance policy . . ." He stared hard at Penny, who was contriving to look innocently ignorant. "Zeb took the policy out only last year. He told me that it was his sole asset, because the house he lives in belongs to the Dimolas and his pension from them stops with his death. He said he wanted to have something to leave to me since I was his only kin and he's got very fond of Bobby . . ." He drew the car up carefully beside Penny's at the Langley cottage and turned off the engine; he looked straight ahead out of the windshield. "All very innocent and understandable really, but it makes one hell of a motive. Or so thinks Birnie, and the word is spreading. I've been getting some mighty peculiar looks from my colleagues the last couple of days." He glanced at her and a sudden grin transformed his face. "But don't look so worried—I didn't do it, honest! I just thought I'd let you know because Birnie and I both now have excellent and opposite reasons for helping you. I'm with you all the way. What's the next step?"

"For me some more talk with Annette Dimola, and then I'm off to Boston. For you, well, you might do some digging around in the local drug scene to see if you can come up with any links to the Masuit estate." Penny was thoughtful. "I've got some ideas about that too. And, oh yes, the mail! Try and find out from the post office when and how that cablegram I sent to your uncle was delivered and particularly if any of the Dimolas were around at the time. One good thing about all this—with Eagle Smith under arrest the murderer must be feeling a whole lot safer; he'll be off guard and less likely to be concerned about what we're up to." They parted amiably.

Penny sought out Annette Dimola on her return to the mansion. "I have to go into Boston," she explained, "but there is one question I wanted to ask you before I took off. The last time we talked you mentioned that Mr. Dimola's brothers were killed in the war. Were they married? And did he have any sisters and, if so, are they married with families?"

Annette looked faintly puzzled but answered readily enough. "No, neither of his brothers was married—they were all pretty young, you realize—and Rinaldo is the sole survivor. There was one sister but she died as a child."

"And how about cousins?"

"None that I know of, and I don't think there are any because I recall, when Steven and Rinaldo were talking about the genealogy, Rinaldo saying something about them being the only branch of the Dimolas left."

"And his parents?"

"Both dead long since, I'm afraid."

"I see, well thank you," Penny said, and left it at that. She stopped at Chase's to gas up before embarking on the Boston trip. There was no sign of Albert and in answer to her honking Mr. Chase came out of the store to serve her. "Hear you're up at the big house now," he remarked as he pumped the gas.

"Yes. Mrs. Rinaldo Dimola has been very kind and hospitable."

His lugubrious face hardened and he bent down to the open window. "Mrs. Spring, you seem to be a nice lady, and folks hereabouts appreciate what you're trying to do for Zeb, so, a word of warning. Don't get taken in by Annette Dimola. She's a schemer if there ever was one. The first Mrs. Dimola—she was a Chase, you know—was a nice lady just like you, and she had the wool pulled over *her* eyes." He snorted gently. "All the time she was thinking Steven and Annette were going to make a match of it—not but what there was plenty who'd have agreed with her, the way they used to go on!—and then, when she was hardly cold in the ground, poor soul, Annette ups and marries the main chance. A proper scandal it was."

Penny tried not to let her surprise show. "But surely Steven Dimola was married about that time too."

"He rushed off to foreign parts, true enough, and when he came back with a wife folks all said it was one of them rebound things. If you ask me, it was the best day's work he ever did." A glow of appreciation appeared in the dark eyes. "Fine figure of a woman, Mrs. Steven is, and sensible too. Has her head on straight, which is more than I can say of some up there. Anyway, thought I'd better say my say so that you won't be taken in like most folks are. Oh, and another thing, young Eagle Smith didn't do that to Zeb; that boy is all hot air, there's no violence in him." He nodded significantly and, stepping back from the car, waved her off.

As Penny settled down to the long dreary drive she chewed on this new nugget of information, which had all the elements of classic tragedy. It might account, she reflected, for whatever lay between Steven and Ann Langley, whose physical resemblance to the slightly older Annette had struck her from the first. Men didn't often change their taste in women, and the Dimola taste ran heavily to blondes. How far had that gone, she wondered, and was the possessive Inga as unaware of it as she appeared to be? She shook herself impatiently; she was getting sidetracked and she needed to think squarely about the main issue so that she could succinctly put the problem for Toby to solve. There was an outside chance that the murder was bound up with Rinaldo's war service in Italy, with one of that group of men, all supposedly dead, who appeared in the photo. But she did not really think so. The striking resemblance of the dentition of the corpse to Rinaldo's own argued for a blood connection—but what kind of connection? A bastard, sired on some Italian girl during the war? And if so, whose? Rinaldo's or one of his dead brother's?

From Zeb's little note to himself it was obvious that he had been thinking along the same lines. The apparent age of the corpse as given in the coroner's report deducted from the present year placed his birthdate *in* the war. Zeb must have seen the corpse—possibly even before the face was mutilated—and seen the resemblance to his hero; but at that point Rinaldo lay stricken (and was that just a coincidence or had something triggered the stroke?), so Zeb was on the horns of a dilemma and in his panic had called her in. His note about Imola—did that represent knowledge or supposition? Whichever it was she felt it was an obvious starting point for Toby, and there she would send him.

She frowned to herself as the great objection to all this supposition weighed on her. Supposing all this was true, what possible threat could the unknown have posed? What threat big enough to drive someone to murder? Illegitimacy was no great thing these days to anyone; it could cause scandal perhaps, blackmail even, but the only one involved enough, fanatical enough about the family honor, to be influenced by such motives was the one man who could not *possibly* have done it, Rinaldo himself. For the rest the arrival of a long-lost bastard might have been an embarrassment but surely nothing more; certainly nothing to warrant murder. And the only other fanatic around was Zeb, who could conceivably murder someone who posed a threat to his hero, but who couldn't possibly have committed the murder either.

Or was that so impossible? For a wild moment her mind toyed with the idea that Zeb's appeal to her had been a demented attempt at a smoke screen, a guilt-ridden "catch-me-if-you-can" challenge. But that was ridiculous too, for Zeb certainly had not bashed his own head in on the bog. Yet, if there *was* a drug angle to the case and Zeb's attack was connected with *that*, then her first idea might not be so ridiculous after all . . . Her thoughts whirled with the complications, and almost thankfully she turned her mind back to dealing with the thickening stream of traffic as the Boston skyline came into view.

A weary time later she was sitting engulfed behind John Everett's big desk, waiting impatiently for the phone to ring. Everett himself was out, busy playing a willing Watson to her Sherlock Holmes, and trying to get a newspaper to transmit a teleprint of the photo she had given him to an Italian counterpart in Bologna. When the telephone did jingle she seized it and felt an overwhelming sense of relief to hear Toby's mellifluous rumble at the other end; it was a very puzzled rumble.

Her own nerves at full jangle, she wasted no time on

polite amenities. "Look, Toby, I'm in deep trouble and urgently need your help, and this call is going to cost John Everett a fortune, so just shut up and listen," she said all in one breath. The rumble assured her resignedly that it wasn't a bit surprised about *that* and to go ahead.

She talked solidly for half an hour, at the end of which, considerably out of breath, she panted, "So you understand what to look for, and how important it all is. If no one remembers Dimola's wartime activities there, try and find out what he did there two years ago; who he saw and so on. And also try to find out what other family members were there too. Got all that?"

Toby, whose photographic memory was renowned, said huffily that he had "got it" long since, but where was he supposed to pick up the telephoto?

She told him and added belatedly, "I hope this isn't going to upset your own plans too much. I wouldn't have bothered you if there had been any other way."

"Nice of you to be so considerate," the phone boomed sarcastically, "but, not to worry; I can't think of a better way to spend my vacation than snooping around a benighted village after some long-forgotten or possibly non-existent scandal, but I'll do what I can. How can I get in touch with you when I have unearthed the closeted skeletons?"

That indeed was a problem. After some rapid thought she gave him John Everett's number and then the Dimola number and Ann's extension. "If it's not something vital," she went on, "call John, and we'll have to fix up something here for him to relay the message to me. If it's something that simply can't wait, call the Dimola number, but if you do that, for God's sake be careful in what you say—it's a case of walls have ears."

"Even if we talk Swahili?" Toby's voice was heavily amused.

"Oh, I never thought of that!" Penny confessed. "Our one joint language that nobody would understand. How clever you are, Toby! So call the Dimolas direct then. And good hunting—and bless you!"

"I'm glad you appreciate it," Toby said. "Bless you too.

And in Heaven's name don't get into any more trouble, it looks as if we've got more than we can handle right now." The line went dead.

Penny smiled at the phone. "He said 'we,' " she said aloud fondly, "he's hooked!"

CHAPTER 12

She dined with John Everett, who was so eager to continue his Watson role, that she set him the task of finding out about Wanda Dimola's background and also to check into the activities of Dimola Enterprises to see if Alexander's picture of his father as a man without archenemies held up. Feeling she had accomplished a lot for one day, she drove back to the Cape through the cold darkness, taking the complicated route to the Dimola mansion with the unerring ease of a homing pigeon.

She arrived to find all the travelers returned and assembled in the huge drawing room. As she stood on the threshold of its brightly lit warmth it was like looking at a scene from an ultrasophisticated stage play. Wanda—a completely changed Wanda—was dominating the scene. Clad in a gold lamé sheath that clung in all the right places to reveal the spectacular figure, she was standing before the roaring blaze in the great fireplace, vivid color in her animated face, her eyes sparkling with mischievous light; her husband and Annette were listening to her, appreciative grins on their faces. Inga was snuggled close to Steven on one of the deep sofas, talking quietly while fussing with his lapels or smoothing his hair, like a mother straightening up her child to have its picture taken. Steven did not seem to mind this fussing in the very least. Ann was sipping a drink, a thoughtful expression on her face, and only Maria on the same sofa was looking worried and unhappy.

At Penny's entrance Wanda stopped in mid-sentence and there was a moment's startled silence, as if they had forgotten all about her, then the men got to their feet and Alexander said cheerfully, "Ah, there you are, Dr. Spring, come on in and have a brandy to shake off the chill of the drive. I hear your worries are over and the case has been solved for you. Quick work by our local police, eh? I expect now you'll be in a hurry to get off to warmer climes."

Penny smiled vaguely at him, accepted the drink and took a seat by the worried-looking Maria. "You mean Eagle Smith? I'm so glad you are all here so that I can talk to you about that. You know him, of course?" She saw Wanda exchange a quick glance with Inga before her husband answered, "Why, no! Why do you think we know him?"

"Oh, being a local boy I thought you almost certainly would." She was smooth. "But I do want to talk to you about him, since I am certain the police have made an honest mistake but one which, in the interests of justice, I am anxious to rectify. The young man is in prison and cannot raise the bail set, $3,000, I understand." She looked at Steven. "I was going to ask you if you would be willing to stand bail for him to get him out."

There was a startled silence, then Steven said in his mild, diffident voice, "Well, of course it is perfectly possible, though I don't quite understand . . ."

Alexander seemed to swell, he glanced angrily at his brother, then at Penny; for the first time he looked dangerous. "Look here, Dr. Spring, what is all this about? Are you trying to implicate *us*, by any chance? If the court has set a high bail it means they consider him dangerous and don't want him out. Why should we interfere?"

"Because, like it or not, you *are* involved," Penny said calmly. "The young man won't talk as long as he is in prison, and I badly need to talk to him. One way or another I intend to get him out, but I thought it would be better for your own local image if *you* did it. There will be a lot of tension in the community over this arrest; the detective in charge of the case has not got him in prison because he thinks he is dangerous, but because he thinks he can break him down there—if he knew the least thing about Indians, he'd know this is a vain hope—and, not being a local man, he does not understand the rest of the situation."

"She's right, you know," Maria said suddenly, "they hate us around here. You could tell that at the inquest. I'd never realized that before, but they do."

"Hate is a strong word," Penny said, though she was glad of the unexpected support. "I think mistrust is perhaps a better one. They're afraid your money and your power could be used to obstruct rather than bring about justice. Eagle Smith may not be blameless in other matters but, so far as the attack on Zeb goes, many—including some of the police—do not think he did it. If you set him at liberty I think it would be a good and wise gesture on your part."

"Then I'll do it," Steven said.

"Just hold on——" Alexander began hotly.

"It is for *me* to say in father's absence," Steven cut him off, and the two brothers glared at one another in sudden mutual antagonism, as Inga plucked nervously at her husband's sleeve. He turned to Penny. "I'll arrange it first thing in the morning."

"Thank you. And, as you've gathered, I do not think the matter is anywhere near closed, so I shall not be leaving. However," she looked over at Annette, who had been totally impassive throughout the exchange, "I feel I have imposed on your hospitality long enough, so now that Ann is back I'll return to the cottage—if that's all right with you?" She looked at Ann, who nodded a startled affirmative. There was a tiny moment of silence before Annette answered, "You're perfectly welcome to stay on here, if you choose, Dr. Spring, but it is entirely up to you."

"Well then, I think I'll go up and pack."—Penny got up briskly, hoping to dissipate some of the tension in the room —"so that I'll be all ready when you want to go, Ann." Maria got up with her. "I think I'll go and sit with father for a while," she announced, and followed Penny out.

When the door was closed on the silent company behind them Maria turned to Penny. "Would you come and see father? I'm worried sick," she said urgently, "I badly need some advice."

Without waiting for a reply she hurried up the grand, marble-balustraded staircase, an intrigued Penny puffing up after her; then along a tapestried and antiqued corridor to two large double doors, where Maria signaled for silence. She slipped inside and a moment later one of the Portuguese maids came out with a shy smile at Penny and motioned her to go in.

Once again she stepped across the threshold into medieval Italy, the only incongruity being that the massive, canopied four-poster bed had been moved over to one side of the room and its place taken by a run-of-the-mill hospital bed with all its accoutrements. Maria was standing by it, looking down at the burly, still figure propped up in a sitting position. She motioned Penny to join her. "He's dozing," she whispered, "but before I wake him there's something I've got to tell you . . . I think I may have done something terrible." And Penny saw there were tears trickling silently down the young face. "The others just treat him like a dummy, but I've been trying to stimulate him by telling him things I thought would interest him, *anything* to get him going again . . . it's so terrible to see him just *lying* there . . ." Her voice choked. "I really thought I was making some progress, he was starting to try and say words again and there even seemed to be some movement in one of his hands. I could tell he *wanted* to get better. It was in his eyes. The doctors said that stroke was so massive it should have killed him, but he is so strong, so determined, that he came out of it. And he gives me this terrific impression of waiting for something. This *was* how he was, I should have said . . ." She gulped. "The other day I was telling him about the inquest and something I said then upset him terribly. The trouble is I don't know what. I was so scared I got Inga, and she was dreadfully cross, but she packed me off and got him calmed down somehow. She's a good sort, she didn't tell the others what I had done. But ever since . . ." Her voice broke again. "It's as if he has given up hope. He isn't eating, he won't *talk* to me anymore. He just lies there with this horrible blank stare. Oh, I'm so frightened . . . !"

"What do you mean, *talk?*" Penny whispered urgently. "Does he actually say things?"

"No, not really talk. It's a sort of signal we've worked out. He can blink his eyelids. But before this he was beginning to try and say things."

"What things?"

"Well, he kept saying what sounded like 'Ann, Ann.' "

"Your step-mother?"

Maria frowned in the dim light. "No, I don't think so, because I asked him if he wanted me to fetch her and he signaled 'no.' "

"Anything else?"

"Nothing that makes sense. He'd say 'end-so' or 'and-so'

over and over. Sometimes it was almost as if he was trying to sing. You know, like 'la-la-la.' "

Penny frowned too, for she could make no sense of it either. As Maria worried on aloud, she looked with compassion at the massive immobile figure on the bed. Rinaldo put her in mind of a fallen oak, for, even in his helpless stillness there still emanated from him an aura of power and solidity. "Does he sleep a lot?" she asked.

"Yes. Lately, since the upset, I think Inga has been keeping him sedated most of the time. Oh, what a fool I am!"

Penny looked at her with curiosity. "I sort of gathered you did not get along too well with your father, yet you seem very concerned about him."

Maria's face became sullen. "Well, that's true enough. When I was little, oh, it was wonderful then, he used to want me with him the whole time, but when I got a bit older, then it was nothing but the damn boys, boys, *boys,* all the time. I didn't seem to count any more; nothing I ever did was right. The only time he ever seemed to notice me was when he'd bawl me out. So . . ."—an expression of satisfaction spread over the vivid face—"I gave him plenty to bawl me out about. I was almost glad when this happened. It was almost like the old days again. He needed me, I'm sure he did—and now . . ." Her face puckered again.

"So you love him very much," Penny murmured. Maria nodded, her eyes blinded with tears.

"Enough to help me get to the bottom of this affair? For I think that is what is upsetting your father."

"You mean about Zeb Grange?"

"No, about the body in the bog. I think your father knows who it is. If you could get him talking again, he might be able to help us."

Maria looked at her in the dim light in startled silence. "I could try . . ." she faltered. Very gently she shook the huge arm. "Poppa, Poppa," she whispered, "it's me, Maria. I've brought a visitor for you."

The dark eyes slowly opened, straining to focus through their drugged fog, and there dawned in them a terrible gleam of frantic hope. The eyes turned painfully and focused on Penny's diminutive figure, but the wild gleam died to be replaced with an awful blankness; if ever Penny had seen Death appear in a man's eyes she saw it now, and recoiled from the terrible message.

"Poppa," Maria went on excitedly, "this is a detective, Dr. Spring, and she wants us to help her with what I was telling you about the other day—the man they found in our bog? You and me together. We can, can't we, Poppa?"

The awful glare still fixed on Penny, the heavy eyelids came down and slowly opened again. Maria gave a little gasp. "He says 'no'!" Then the eyelids came down again and remained shut.

"If I could talk to him when he isn't sedated, I think I could convince him . . ." Penny started to say, when the door opened and Annette's slim figure was outlined against the brighter light of the hallway. For a moment she just stood there, then came purposefully in. "What are you doing? What is the meaning of this?" she demanded.

Maria started to bluster. "I brought Dr. Spring to see father. I thought it would cheer him up to see a new face . . ."

Annette advanced into the circle of the bedside light and Penny could see she was coldly and furiously angry. "As usual you take a lot too much on yourself, Maria. You'd better go. I will stay with him now. Dr. Spring, I understood you were going to pack. Ann is waiting for you downstairs. Perhaps you should do that. Good-bye." Her tone was cutting, the hazel eyes hard and unforgiving.

Maria started to open her mouth to argue, but Penny seized her arm and squeezed; a strategic retreat was in order. "Yes, of course, I'm sorry," she muttered and propelled the unwilling girl toward the door.

Once outside she relaxed her grip but said urgently, "That was most unfortunate, but from now on, Maria, you'll have to be extra careful. Say nothing about what you have told me to *anyone,* keep a very close eye on your father, and if the chance comes get him talking again, but do it in secret. Also, be sure and check with the doctor on the drugs Inga has been giving your father; she is only a nurse, after all, and may not know as much about it as she thinks she does. Do your brothers sit with your father ever?"

"Steven does sometimes, but Alexander is so busy that

he only pops in for a few minutes at a time, when one of us is there."

"And how does your father seem then, any different?"

Maria hesitated for a moment. "I can tell a lot from Poppa's eyes, and up to the last upset I would have said that what he was feeling for Alexander was—pity."

"Pity!" It was the last thing Penny had expected. "Can you explain that?"

"Well, I put it down to the fact that he does have all the business worries now, and of course Wanda is such a constant pain in the neck."

"And with Steven?"

Maria shrugged, "I don't know, really. Even though he's always made such a big thing about Steven being the elder, Poppa has never been as close to him as to Alexander. Steven's got a lot of the cold New England blood of the Chases in him"—she smiled suddenly—"and, as such, has always been a bit of a mystery to us hot-blooded Italians."

"I have one more question to ask you, and don't be offended by it, I just have to clear some ground. You are very much with and of your generation—have you ever used drugs?"

Maria grinned knowingly at her. "Oh, I've smoked plenty of pot in my time, in fact I nearly got bounced out of college for it."

"How about pills?"

"I've popped a few," she admitted, "just to be maty with my first husband, he was a great pill-popper. But I could not get on with them, they made me sick to my stomach, so I cut out on them."

"And your brothers?"

"No *way!* They'd have been too afraid of Poppa."

"How about Wanda? You know the signs—have you seen them on her?"

Maria became serious. "It has crossed my mind," she admitted. "Those wild swings of mood she has. Could be her frustrated artistic temperament, of course . . . she was a class-A nitwit to give up *her* career on Alex's account . . . but, yes, she could be a user. Though God knows how she'd ever get hold of the stuff in this household."

Penny said nothing, but reflected that this was an answer she could readily supply. "And how about Inga?"

"Heavens, no! Inga's a health freak. Lectures on smoking, drinking, drug taking, etc., etc., to order. Always jogging and working out. She wouldn't go near the stuff. No, her only vices are eating—which you may have noticed she does a lot of—and Steve, poor lad! Steve'll never be without his mum while Inga's around . . ."

Ann's clear voice came floating up the stairs. "Is that you, Dr. Spring? Are you ready to go?"

Penny started guiltily. "In just a few minutes," she called back, and with a reassuring nod at Maria scuttled off to fling her things in a bag.

On the short ride back to the cottage she apologized to Ann for the delay, then added, "Look, my dear, if it will make things awkward for you up at the house having me stay on, I wish you'd say so. I can easily go to a local motel, you know. I don't want to make any trouble for you with the Dimolas."

"No, I'm sure they understand," Ann said in an absent voice, "and actually, with everything that's been going on, I'm glad to have some company in the house. It gets so lonely in the winter."

The loneliness of the dark, pine-enshrouded cottage emphasized her words as she shut off the engine. The sea mist had come again, and Penny was reminded forcibly of her first encounter with it as they unloaded the bags and groped their way to the darkened house. Ann fumbled with the keys and, flinging open the door, reached inside to put on the lights. "I'll be so glad to see little Penny tomorrow . . ." she began to say, when she stopped dead, and Penny peering over her shoulder saw the cause: the visible parts of the cottage were in considerable disarray.

"You haven't been back here, have you?" Ann asked uncertainly.

"No," Penny said, and there was a trickle of fear up her spine, "not since we left together."

"Then it looks as if someone has ransacked the place," Ann quavered, and there was an edge of panic in her voice. "What on earth could they have been looking for?"

CHAPTER 13

Sir Tobias Glendower—that archaeologist extraordinary—
was feeling not unpleased by the turn of events. His Italian
trip so far had not lived up to expectation; the problems he
had been invited to solve on his Italian colleague's dig
he had found existed mainly in the mind of the latter and
had been rapidly dealt with. The weather had not been up
to par, he had found no thrilling new vintages, and he had
been missing Penny's stimulating, if irritating, company
more than he cared to admit. Now, after that momentous
transatlantic call, his vacation had taken on new life and
purpose, and he conveniently swamped any guilt feelings
he had had about not following her to America by the
stronger feelings of annoyance and being put upon by her
demands. From now on, if anything untoward happened,
he could firmly put the blame on her.

Transportation was no problem since he had driven in
his own car from England; the Bentley was old but comfortable and trouble-free, which suited Toby excellently
on all counts, for he was not mechanically minded. It
purred under his accustomed touch as he drove southeast
from Bologna over the old Via Emilia of the Romans,
the long line of the Apennines stretching into misty blue
distances on his right hand. Imola was new territory for
him, though he knew its history in a vague sort of way:
devastated by Justinian for some obscure reason, rebuilt
by the Lombards, an independent commune in the Middle
Ages (had it been Guelph or Ghibelline?—he didn't really
know), finally part of the Papal States under the iron hand
of the Borgias. He was a little uncertain where he should
start his strange hunt, but felt that a small place would
easily yield its secrets to his questing eye. "*This* time,"
he told himself firmly, "I shall start where any scholar
should start—with the records. That was my big mistake

in Pergama. If I'd checked the written sources at the beginning we wouldn't have had half as much trouble."

As he drove into the outskirts of Imola, however, the first misgivings stirred in him; it was far bigger than he had imagined. He passed some factories for agricultural implements, a large pottery works, and a larger natural gas installation. In fact Imola had all the earmarks of a bustling North Italian manufacturing center. With unerring instinct he drove toward the ancient heart of the town and with some difficulty found a parking spot for the Bentley in the busy, narrow streets. "Hmm," he instructed himself, as he uncoiled his lanky, stooped frame from behind the wheel, "get the feel of the place—a good move number one!"

He dutifully inspected the medieval citadel, a couple of fifteenth-century palazzi and the late Gothic church of Saint Domenico. He skipped the cathedral (rebuilt in the eighteenth century) and made for the museum where he looked at a fine ceramic collection, some indifferent paintings, and a sad jumble of early antiquities. As he gazed at a case full of Roman bric-a-brac it occurred to him that he had seen no sign of the medieval tower featured in the rather fuzzy photo that had come over the teleprinter. He cast a glance around for the most amiable-looking of the museum guards, knowing from past experience that they were often more than willing for a chat to relieve the aching boredom of their job. He selected a round-faced, portly, fair-haired man for his prey, approached him and offered the photo. "Per favore, dove il torre?" he asked. The guard peered at the fuzzy outlines of the photo, a puzzled expression on his face. "Non è qui," he said cheerfully.

"Not here! But this was taken in Imola in 1944," Toby protested.

"It's not here," the guard said, firmly this time.

"But it has an inscription right on it. Colle d'Imola, 1944!"

"Oh, *Colle* d'Imola," the guard corrected. "Well, that's not here." He jerked his head vaguely over his shoulder. "It's about ten kilometers up in the hills, a small village." He looked at the photo again. "You were here in the war then?"

Toby shook his head; although he did not look it, with

his silver hair, spindly shanks and his face of an aged baby, he had been too young for World War II. "Where would I find the local records?"

This appeared to stump the guard. "Records?" he echoed. "What kind of records?"

"Oh, land records, births, marriages and deaths—that kind of thing."

The guard shrugged. "The municipal offices, I suppose, but they do not go back very far. They were all burned by the Germans."

"Oh dear!" Toby said dismally, his dreams of instant success shattering. "Are you sure about that?"

"Quite sure." The guard was cheerful again. "Imola was in the thick of things; the Germans took it, the Americans took it, the Germans took it back, the Americans came back again and the partisans were in and out fighting everyone. Oh, it was a bad time here and no mistake!"

"And how about Colle d'Imola—would their records be there or here?"

The guard shrugged. "I don't know. Why don't you go there and ask. You speak Italian very well," he added encouragingly.

"Is there an hotel I could stay in up there," Toby asked.

A delighted expression came into the guard's face. "No hotel—only here are hotels—but you perhaps could stay with my uncle Enrico. He runs a little inn in the village. He does not cater to tourists but he just might put you up. You like good Italian wine? My uncle, he has a good cellar." He winked.

Toby's small ears pricked up. "Has he indeed! And how might I find him?"

The guard told him and added, "Tell Enrico, Giuseppe sent you—he will treat you well."

Toby thanked him and offered a tip which was brushed gracefully aside with "It has been a pleasure to talk to you, signore. Give my regards to my uncle."

To be thorough Toby checked in at the local municipal offices, only to find that the guard's fears had been correct. All old records, with trifling exceptions, had been destroyed during the war; the only ones available were from 1946 onward. On the records for Colle d'Imola they were a little vague; some were kept in the village, others here, and they could neither find them nor tell him anything more. With the sinking feeling that his task was going to be a lot more difficult than he had anticipated, Toby thanked them and, after a brief consultation with his road map, set off for Colle d'Imola.

At least, he reflected, small places usually had long memories and that might be in his favor, and equally, since the village was off the well-beaten tourist track, if the Dimolas had been there fairly recently they and their activities might be well remembered.

The road shook off the tattered outskirts of Imola and began to climb steeply into the Apennine foothills, and he could soon see the rose and ocher roofs of the village peeping out through gaps in a very decrepit medieval fortification wall that encircled it on its hilltop. He could still see no sign of the tower. There was a yawning gap in the walls where the original gates used to be and he drove through it into an archetypical little sun-drenched village square, a small fountain dribbling halfheartedly in its very center.

One side of the square was taken up by a small palazzo, its sixteenth-century face much pockmarked by shell and bullet scars and most of its shutters closed. Sticking up from one corner of it he saw what was left of the tower, showing like a huge broken fang, the whole of its upper part destroyed. The rest of the square bore similar marks of destruction; old stone facades patched and repaired with brick and stucco, old roofs interspersed with ones of newer, less decorative, tile. There were some gaps where wild flowers and weeds ran riot over rotting beams and timbers. Colle d'Imola had evidently never quite recovered from the devastating steel hand of modern warfare.

He located the small inn sign hanging over an equally scarred and patched building in the square opposite the palazzo. There were only two old Cinquecentos parked in the square, and he felt absurdly conspicuous parking the Bentley in front of the inn. His arrival had not gone unremarked, for, in an instant, a small gaggle of children appeared apparently out of nowhere and stood gazing in wide-eyed amazement as he climbed out. Never at his best with children, he glared threateningly at them with icy blue eyes and rumbled, "The first one who touches that car will grow horns—understood?" There was a communal nodding of heads as they retreated a step or two backward, and with another glare at them he ducked under the low portal of the inn.

Inside, apart from the age-old fragrance of wine, the twentieth century had triumphed completely. Bright red plastic-topped tables stood around surrounded by sticky looking varnished chairs, but it was evident from the wear on the brightly patterned floor linoleum that the patrons of the establishment spent most of the time propped up at the wooden bar, which was the only item in the place that had an older, more substantial and battered look. Even here the hand of the twentieth century was evident, for, angled high in one corner of it, was a small television set. The place was completely empty, and only when he got to the bar and stood peering uncertainly around did the bead curtain that stood off to one side of it part and a small portly man emerge. He looked at Toby with a hard, unfriendly eye. "What can I do for you?"

Feeling ridiculous, Toby muttered, "Your nephew Giuseppe sent me. He thought you might be able to put me up for a few days."

"We do not cater to tourists. There are hotels in Imola; you would be more comfortable there."

"I am not a tourist," Toby persisted, "I have some business in Colle d'Imola and I would prefer to stay here. I understand from Giuseppe that you have a fine cellar."

The man relaxed a little but his face was still guarded. "Oh, you like wine, signore? What can I get you. We have . . ." and he named several indifferent wines that Toby was well aware were popular and overpriced vintages foisted off on tourists.

Toby brought his big guns to bear. He looked disappointed and then said deliberately, "Well, no, my taste runs more to a good Barolo, preferably the '70 or '72 vintages, or possibly, if that is too far north for you, some Lambrusca. Or a Sangiovese—'77 was a good year there, but that's a bit new—I don't suppose you have any of the '60 vintages left? Or, even better, I would like to try a good local wine if such exists."

Enrico looked at him with dawning respect. "I see you know your wines," he said grudgingly, and after a moment's hesitation produced a dusty unmarked bottle from under the bar. "Perhaps you would care to try this." He poured some of the blood-red liquid into a glass and pushed it across the bar to Toby, who picked it up, looked critically at its color, sniffed its bouquet, took a small sip and rolled it expertly around his tongue and then took a bigger sip. His round blue eyes went a little rounder behind his glasses. "Mm," he said thoughtfully, "a cross between Barolo and a Lachrima Christi, but more full-bodied and with a taste of, mm, let's see, mountain flowers. Very good." He looked questioningly at Enrico, whose face broke into a delighted grin. "Yes, it is the soil around here. The old Lombard vines and the soil make for full-bodied wines . . . ." The ice was broken. He poured himself a glass and held it up to Toby. "See the color—the color of good blood! *Salute!*"

They had several more and talked wine for a good half hour, then Enrico said casually, "You said you had business here, signore? It is not often an Inglese has business in Colle d'Imola."

Toby hedged. "It is really on behalf of an American friend, concerning a family with connections here. I happened to be vacationing near here, so she asked my help. Would you be able to put me up for a day or two. I'd prefer to be on the spot rather than drive from Imola."

The wine had made Enrico amiable, but he was still cautious. "Our guest room is not very modern, although the bed is comfortable, and while my wife is a good cook our fare is simple and 'del paese,' but, so long as you understand that, you would be welcome as a guest. Would you like to see the room?"

To Toby food was only important insofar as it complemented whatever he was drinking, and his heedlessness of creature comforts was so marked as to drive Penny, who was very fond of hers, to distraction. So he said quickly, "Yes, I would—and the rest sounds excellent. What are your rates?"

Enrico blandly named a sum triple what he would normally have charged, expecting some lively argument, but to his utter astonishment Toby, who had never had to think twice about money in his whole life, instantly said, "Well, that sounds very reasonable. Shall we go?" They negotiated the bead curtain and a flight of narrow stairs and Toby was introduced to the guest chamber, a small, spotlessly clean room dominated by a huge double bed and wardrobe, with an old-fashioned washstand and a chair squeezed between their bulk. Toby thought about asking for a table, and then decided there was no possible room for it, so he nodded a cheerful approbation. He was then trailed downstairs to the family living quarters, where he was duly introduced to an equally plump Mrs. Enrico, who was busy at the stove with two small children clinging to her skirts. "This gentleman speaks very good Italian," Enrico said warningly, "and he'll be staying with us for a few days."

Mrs. Enrico dutifully nodded, but the news did not seem to fill her with any great joy. "Your baggage, signore?"

"Out in the car." They emerged into the bright sunlight to find the gaggle of children now closely pressed about the car but still not touching, their numbers augmented by one or two interested adults. "Er, is there any way to keep them off?" Toby enquired.

"Leave it to me," Enrico said. He raised his voice in thunder and made a short speech, the gist of which was that they were being honored by the visit of a distinguished English milord, and that if anyone put so much as a fingermark on the milord's car they would have to answer to him as headman of the village. The crowd retreated a respectful distance, but continued to stand and stare as Toby's elegant, if worn, suitcases were disgorged from the Bentley and taken inside. Some of the men showed an inclination to follow them in but Enrico shut the door firmly on them with a "Closed—come back later." Then turned to Toby, "We have time for another glass or two before the meal is ready, signore, if you wish."

"An excellent idea," Toby said. "Do you have whites as well as red from the region?"

"Yes, but not as good as the red, but anyway you would like to try, eh?" Toby nodded as a teen-aged boy appeared and took his bags away. "My fourth son," Enrico informed him. "I have eight children." Seeing the almost comical dismay on Toby's face he grinned reassuringly and said, "But you can take your meals in the parlor beneath the guest room. If you are not used to children, our family table may be too lively for you."

Toby received this news with relief and they settled to a bottle of white. "Now, Signor Glendower," Enrico said, more firmly this time, "you said you have business in the region. Perhaps I could assist you?"

"I certainly hope so," Toby agreed, "since I am sure this excellent inn is the center of the life of the village. Incidentally, here is the money for a week's lodging in advance."

Enrico pocketed the money with satisfied alacrity but went back to the main point. "And what do you want to know?"

"Well, it is in connection with the Dimola family and the war."

Enrico's brows knitted. "D'Imola?" he said, and with him the apostrophe was clear, "but there is no one of that name here, nor has been in my memory. You are sure your business is here and not in Imola itself?"

"Quite sure," Toby said, with more certainty than he felt. "My enquiry is concerning a Dimola who was here during the war. You were here then?"

"Oh, yes"—Enrico's face was somber—"I was just a boy; I am the youngest of my family, but I was here. And a hard time of it we had, I can tell you. My father was inn-keeper here and those—Germans took him as a hostage and shot him, because they said he aided the partisans hiding out in the mountains. We had it all—shellings, bombings, people taken away and never seen again; even the women . . ." His tone was venomous. "Even foreigners like the Amalfis—no one was spared."

"The Amalfis?"

"The padrones here, the owners of the palazzo. Brought in by the Borgias and we've never been rid of them since," he said with surprising bitterness.

Toby quietly marveled to himself at the long arm of rustic history; an aristocratic family brought in four hundred years ago and yet never accepted by the local people. "The palazzo looked deserted to me," he remarked.

"Oh, no. The Contessa lives there—the Contessa Anna-Maria Amalfi—if you can call it living!" Enrico said with a scornful laugh, "though there is nothing much left for the Amalfis to be proud of."

"The man I am enquiring about was evidently stationed

here during the war. His name was Dimola, Rinaldo Dimola."

A loud crash made them both jump, and they turned to see that Mrs. Enrico, who had entered with a trayful of glasses in hand, had just dropped it on the floor and was now gazing at them with wide-eyed consternation.

CHAPTER 14

"*Church* records? No, Signor Glendower, I don't think so."

It was some time later and the small inn was crowded with thirsty clients. Toby had dined in thankful, solitary splendor in the evidently unused parlor of the inn. It was hideous in magenta plush and carved oak, but he had been happy to see a small square antique table—hurriedly cleared of a vast collection of family photographs—at which he had dined seated in another family relic, a high-backed armchair. The dinner had been excellent; a minestrone, so thick the spoon could stand up in it, a dish of buttered linguine, and then a delectable gorgonzola and raisins to go with another flask of the excellent red wine. Listening to the continuing roar of Enrico's prolific family at table, even muted as it was by the thick doors of the inn, he had counted his blessings and had eaten heartily.

More than replete, he had staggered out to join the evening throng at the bar, and was now propped up against it, puffing on his pipe and listening intently to the buzz of conversation around him. Enrico and his wife were so busy serving the curious throng that it had been some time before Toby could get back to his questions.

He knew full well he was the main object of attention, though rustic courtesy was inhibiting the clientele from commenting about him openly since Enrico had pointedly introduced him as the "milord Inglese who speaks Italian." Every time he opened his mouth, in fact, there was almost instant silence as they hung on his words. It certainly should shake forth something, if there was anything to be shaken, he reflected.

Enrico elaborated on his answer to Toby's question. "The church was shelled—it lies behind the palazzo. The priest was taken as a hostage too and died in a German labor camp. We have a new little church, and you could ask the priest, but I do not think anything remains."

114

"How about old Giovanni?" a heavily mustached villager put in.

"Or the Contessa," said another pale-faced man, and there was a communal snigger.

"Giovanni?" Enrico mused. "Yes, that is possible. He was the verger here then—lost a leg in the shelling. He is very old and a little . . ." He touched his temple significantly. "He has become almost a recluse since the last priest arrived—they do not get on. But it is true he might remember from the old times."

"Where can I find him to talk to him?"

"Domani, tomorrow. My wife will have to go with you. He would not talk to a stranger, but she is his great-niece, so he will talk to her." And with that Toby had to be content.

He circulated among the older men, dropping the name of Rinaldo Dimola to no good effect. Some vaguely recalled the name but could or would not remember anything else; only the pale-faced man had any suggestion of worth. He sidled up to Toby. "You should go and see the Contessa," he whispered. "She was well acquainted with the soldati americani *and* the soldati tedeschi *and* the partisans." He added, with a knowing wink, "She knew a lot about men."

The next morning Toby loped off rather uncomfortably by the side of Mrs. Enrico. It was evident from the loud argument he had heard between his host and his wife that she was an unwilling guide. As they walked through the small twisting streets of the village, she kept darting little nervous glances at him, and it was plain to him that the name of Dimola was of far more significance to her than to her husband. Not for the first time he fervently wished Penny were here—most women made him uneasy, and he hadn't the faintest idea how to go about unlocking Mrs. Enrico's tongue.

They arrived at a very tumbledown cottage, and her knocking and calling finally brought forth a very old, bald-headed and almost toothless man, who glared at Toby. She shoved a tureen of soup she had been carrying into the ancient hands and began a heated, low-toned conversation with him. With a sinking feeling Toby anticipated having the door slammed in their faces and groped for the comfort of his pipe and tobacco pouch. At the sight of the latter a gleam of sudden hunger leaped into the old man's eyes, and Toby quickly held it out to him. The old man grabbed it, gave a toothless smile, and with a sudden movement motioned them to come in. Once inside, he closed the door and carefully locked them in the cluttered room.

"Would you please ask him," Toby said to his unwilling intermediary, "if he knows whether any of the church records were saved and where I could find them." The old man was busy lighting up a blackened clay pipe, an expression of near rapture on his seamed face. "He asks what you want to know for," Mrs. Enrico said sullenly.

"I just want to see them, just to look at them." Toby was patient. He had a sudden inspiration. "If he can show me anything of any worth to me, I'll buy him five hundred grams of pipe tobacco."

A sly expression crossed the old man's face and he muttered something to his niece. "He says how about a kilo," she said uncomfortably.

"*If* he has anything useful to me," Toby said firmly, "that is a promise."

The old man gave a quick nod and, seizing his crutch, hobbled into the back of the cottage. After some minutes he emerged clutching awkwardly a bulky package wrapped in yellowed and tattered newspaper. "The priest must not know," he addressed Toby directly for the first time; "he is a stranger and a heretic besides and has no business here."

"Anything you say," Toby agreed amiably and took the package from the trembling hands. Inside were three registers, heavily scorched at the edges and with spots of blue-green mildew blotching the covers. "They were all I could save," old Giovanni said sadly.

With mounting excitement, Toby strode over to the door, unlocked and flung it open to let in the pale sunshine. To his companions' amazement he squatted happily down on the threshold and started to examine the registers. Two he rapidly discarded as being too early, the third looked more promising, starting as it did in 1910. He leafed rapidly through until he reached the war years and then began examining the pages minutely.

The record keeping of the old village priest had been

haphazard; births, marriages and deaths were all entered as they occurred and were not separated out. He also wrote a very crabbed hand which did not help. 1943 yielded nothing, and the damage done by the damp to the entries for 1944 made them almost illegible, but Toby kept doggedly on at it item by item, the two villagers hovering over his shoulder like interested vultures. Suddenly a name leaped out at him from the very bottom of a scorched and mildewed page. "Sposata," it read, "the 16th March 1944. Rinaldo Dimola, bachelor di Boston, Massachusetts, and Christiana Amalfi, spinster, di Colle d'Imola . . ." Toby leaped to his feet in excitement.

"Mother of God," said Mrs. Enrico, reeling back, "so he *did* marry her!"

At the same time Toby was enjoying his leisurely dinner at Colle d'Imola, Penny was hastening toward an important rendezvous which she fervently hoped would do something to elucidate the labyrinth of doubts and suspicions in which she was totally enmeshed. Information had been piling up and all of it was puzzling.

Ann's immediate reaction to the sacking of her cottage had been strange. Though she had been frightened by it she had been adamant that neither the police nor the Dimolas be informed. Nothing was missing, she averred, and to make a fuss about it would only result in more unpleasant publicity, and she was afraid to put her job in jeopardy. Penny could understand that, but could not help wondering if Ann knew the identity of the intruder and was not as honest about there being nothing missing as she maintained. But who or what could it be?

A call to John Everett from the phone booth at Chase's had garnered another pile of information. On the surface Alexander's statement about his father's business activities appeared correct; there had been no scandals, no activities that would have put him on a collison course with the Syndicate, and the only really interesting nugget had been that in the past two years Rinaldo had not been as aggressive as of yore, and that he had been leaving more and more of the actual running of things to Alexander.

Everett had a further interesting item; Maria Dimola's

second husband had briefly worked in the business, but had been fired and there had been some talk of a hushed-up embezzlement.

He also had garnered a lot of information on Wanda Dimola, none of which added up to very much. Her parents ran an Italian delicatessen in the Bronx. She had started in Off-Broadway shows, and at the time of meeting and marrying Alexander had had her first Broadway part; she had also made several TV commercials. She had had one minor brush with the police when they had raided a pot party in Greenwich Village, but that was all.

Since her affluent marriage she had appeared happy to live the life of a rich socialite in Wellesley, where she was understandably a leading light in amateur theatricals for the Junior League and similar organizations. The only sour note was that she did not care for her in-laws, particularly her young mother-in-law, and that her enforced exile on the Cape was not pleasing to her. John Everett had culled his information from several sources, so Penny had no reason to doubt it, though it added up to a big zero.

She had called the hospital to be told there was no change in Zeb's condition and she had heard nothing further from Carson Grange. So now her main hopes for a break were pinned on Eagle Smith. A curt phone call from Steven Dimola had informed her that bail was being arranged for the boy and that he should be liberated that day, and Penny, anticipating that Eagle might very well not want to talk to *her,* had already done some good groundwork in going to see his mother.

She had found her in a small cottage on the outskirts of Masuit; a mixed breed, as were so many of the Wampanoags, with worry writ large in every line of her dusky face. Long and soothingly had Penny talked to her, as she had talked so many times over so many years in faraway places to mothers troubled over wayward sons in a changing world. She had talked not only of Eagle Smith but of Indians in general, and of her own not inconsiderable championship of Indians' rights. When she left, she did so with the firm knowledge that if Mrs. Smith had any influence at all over her militant son that influence would be used on her behalf.

Arriving for the second time that day at the little Smith cottage, the door was opened to her by Eagle himself. He was tall, with the long straight black hair, broad cheekbones and aquiline nose of the Indian; apart from his skin color, which was wrong, he was the very picture of an old-time Wampanoag brave. His face was totally impassive, but he motioned her to come in and Mrs. Smith rose to greet her with a nervous smile. "I have told him all you said to me this morning," she said. "He will listen to you."

"Good." Penny was blunt. She sat down and looked squarely at the boy, who had also sat down without saying a word. "Now, I will not beat about the bush. If you do not know it already, you know now that I am no enemy to your people or to your cause—quite the opposite in fact. I persuaded Mr. Steven Dimola to put up the bail for you because—whatever else you may have been up to—I am convinced you had no part in the attack on Zeb Grange. Nor are you going to be 'railroaded' for it; not only I, but others involved in the case also are going to see to that. I say this because if you are thinking of setting yourself up as an Indian martyr this is the wrong time and the wrong cause. I hope you see this, because I am going to ask you some questions which are of great importance to me and an answer to them will not trap you in any shape, manner or form. O.K.?"

He nodded but did not speak.

"All right. Did you find Zeb face down in that bog and did you turn him over?"

He nodded slowly.

"Did you notice the broken whisky bottle?"

A slight smile touched his firm-lipped mouth and he nodded again.

"Did my coming scare you off and was it you I heard in the bushes?"

Another nod.

"I won't ask why you were scared to be seen there by me. I think in the light of everything else that's pretty evident, but did *you* see anyone else on the bog before you found Zeb, or did you hear any noise of the assault?"

"No"—he spoke for the first time and his voice was surprisingly deep—"I saw no one nor did I hear anything."

"Where were you coming from when you found him?"
His face closed up and he just sat staring at her.

This was obviously a sore point, so Penny thought quickly. "All right, if you won't answer that, let me tell you what I think. *Something* scared off the would-be murderer before he had time to finish the little scenario he had planned. I think you were in the barn and I can guess why. I think the something may have been the creaking of the barn door either as you came out or went in—most barn doors do creak and this is something I can easily check. Were you in the barn?"

He just smiled.

"Did you meet someone in the barn or were you planning to meet someone?" The smile faded and he shook his head almost with impatience.

"The police think you used both the barn and the excavation site as drop points," Penny said deliberately. "Presumably they have some evidence to back this up, I don't know, but that is another affair and not my concern. My guess is that you never actually met your customer but you do know his or her identity. It would save me some time if you would give me the name—I swear I would not reveal it to the police."

Slowly he shook his head and stood up. "I bore no love toward Grange but I did not do this to him, nor do I know who did. I have said all I can say. It is useless to ask me more."

Penny sighed and stood up also. "There is a murderer loose, a murderer who has tried twice, succeeded once and may well try again. Bear that in mind, and if you have something more you can tell me you know where to find me."

On her way home she detoured by the Grange house and stopped to examine the cranberry barn which, somewhat to her surprise, she found to be unlocked. The doors, as predicted, creaked loudly on their rusty iron hinges, and she went in to survey a dusty collection of cranberry boxes, old scoops, sacking, and the general miscellanea that goes with a cranberry harvest. There were a lot of footprints in the dust of the floor, but whatever the police had found there to put their suspicions on Eagle Smith was now obscured, and after a few minutes of halfhearted searching she gave it up and drove back in a slightly depressed frame of mind to the Langley cottage.

Reaching it, she was amazed to hear joyous squeals and peals of laughter coming from inside. She opened the door on a startling sight. Ann, her face flushed, her eyes sparkling with laughter, was sitting on the couch. Crawling around the floor was Carson Grange, one small dark-haired boy and one small fair-haired girl squealing with delight on his back, as he pitched from side to side making loud neighing sounds. He looked up as Penny came in and, with an extra loud whinny, reared up and gently deposited his charges on the couch. "Hi there," he grinned, "I've been waiting for you, and, as you see, these two varmints lassoed me into action. Came to report to the commander in chief," and he smartly saluted her to the delighted giggles of the children.

His own spirits seemed so high that the thought flashed through Penny's mind that he might be drunk, but the sense of general euphoria in the room after the depression of the past few days brought an answering smile to her own lips. "Well, out with it then, Officer Grange!" she said. "I could use some good news."

The smile lingered on his lips but died out of his eyes as he reached into a pocket of his uniform jacket which was draped over a chair. "I typed it out for you, the info you asked for, I mean," he said carefully, avoiding her eyes. "I think you'll find it interesting. Has there been any word from Italy?"

"Not yet. It's a bit soon to expect any, but Toby Glendower will be in touch as soon as he has anything—you can depend on it."

The phone started to ring. "That might be him now—shall I get it?" Penny said. Ann nodded.

She went into Ann's room and picked up the phone. "Dr. Spring here."

The voice at the other end was scarcely above a strained whisper, but every melodic syllable was clear and separate. "I've got to talk to you," it said. "It's very urgent. There's something I think you should know, but I don't want *anyone* else to. This is Wanda Dimola. I'll meet you tomorrow morning at nine—Zeb Grange's house, the museum room. Please be there!"

"Well of course I will, but why not now . . .?" Penny began to say, then realized she was talking to empty air. Wanda Dimola had hung up.

CHAPTER 15

"You mean she died!" There was dismay in Toby Glendower's voice as his wonderful discovery crumbled into dust. A conference was underway in the overcrowded parlor of the inn—the participants Enrico, a nervous but self-important Mrs. Enrico and Toby. "Oh, yes"—Mrs. Enrico was the spokesman, though she kept darting little nervous glances at her husband, as if seeking his moral support and approbation—"it was not more than a year after this marriage, certainly before May of '45 when the war ended, and long after *he* had left. It is a very sad story now I think of it, signore."

"If you could tell it from the beginning, then perhaps I could understand better." Toby was terrified that she might suddenly dry up on him again.

"If you wish, but you must understand I was very young at the time and all I know comes from my mother, rest her soul! and my aunt, who was a maid at the palazzo then. It is like a fairy story, signore, a sad fairy story. Two sisters in love with the young American officer and none of us knowing for sure which one of them he preferred—Anna-Maria, the present Contessa, who was always so proud and so lively, or Christiana, the quiet one. Both of them were beautiful then in quite different ways, and when the Americans came and took the village from the Germans he —this Rinaldo Dimola—was billeted in the palazzo. In the war things happened so quickly . . ." She stopped a moment and sighed. "Then his unit moved out and there was a counterattack. The Germans came back. Oh, that was a terrible time! They took hostages away with them, the priest, your papa"—she turned to her husband—"the Amalfi sisters, and others; all so that the village would be afraid to fight any more. Then . . ." She looked helplessly at her husband. "I am not sure about the next."

Enrico took up the story. "The Germans were retreating

by then, and one of the partisan units raided their column —they were trying to save my father—they got the Amalfis back and took them off up into the hills. *She* did not come back until several months after the war ended—even after the Japanese had given in I think it was—the Contessa, that is. She came back with the partisan leader who was her lover, and her baby, and they said Christiana had died of the ill treatment of the Germans and the hardships after. The Contessa said she'd been buried in the forest, but she put up a beautiful memorial to her in the churchyard; you can see it for yourself, signore. Then they left again and we did not see her for several years. When she came back there was no more partisan leader, but since then, oh, many, many men at the palazzo."

"But then *he* came back," his wife interrupted, and her husband looked surprised.

"I didn't know that!" he exclaimed.

"Oh, yes—many months after the war it was. He came to the palazzo; it was after the Contessa had left again. My aunt told him of Christiana and he carried on like a wild man. He was much changed, my aunt said, gaunt like a wolf. He had been a prisoner of the Germans and wounded besides. When she took him to see the memorial he flung himself on it like a madman and wept. She thought he would kill himself right then and there. But he went away, and now you, signore, tell me he became a great man."

"But he returned here two years ago—you must have heard that then," Toby put in.

She looked startled. "I know nothing of that. My aunt left the palazzo many years ago—such goings-on she could not stand! And as the money got less, the Contessa got worse—such a temper!"

"Didn't he come to the inn to make enquiries?" Toby appealed to Enrico.

"No, he did not come here." Enrico knitted his brows. "But I do seem to recall . . . there are always some tourists that find their way here in summer, you see . . . I can't be sure."

"Would there be someone in the palazzo who would know?"

Enrico shrugged. "Perhaps. But the Contessa no longer

has a servant—only she would know, and she no longer sees anyone but the priest."

"And about the baby you mentioned—what happened to it?"

"Oh, Lorenzetto!" Enrico laughed scornfully. "Best not to ask. Like his mother, that one, and a bane to her just as she has always been to us."

"And his father?"

The peasant faces on either side of him closed up. "She said it was the partisan Lorenzo's child," Enrico said shortly. "She said they were married, but there were many who said it was a German's bastard; the Contessa was not fussy so long as a man attracted her. That is all I know."

"And this Lorenzetto—where is he now?"

Enrico shrugged. "He comes and he goes. He has not been seen in the village for a long time. I do not know where he is or what he does—nor do I care." His tone was bitter.

"Well, I am much indebted to you for all this information," Toby said dolefully, for he did not see how it made any sense at all. "I think I had better go into Imola and see if I can pick up traces of Mr. Dimola's visit there. If I can pin down the time of it maybe someone in the village will remember, and then I had better pay the priest a visit. I suppose it will mean making the rounds of all the hotels in Imola." He sighed heavily.

Enrico looked relieved. "Yes, a trip to Imola, excellent! There are many interesting things to see there. As to the hotels, I think there is only one he would have stayed at: the Olympia on Via Pisacane; try there."

Before he set off, Toby put in a call to Penny to report his findings and his plans. "I thought I was on to something when I found that marriage record," he said in an aggrieved tone, "but now I don't see it gets us one bit further ahead. The poor girl was dead and gone before Dimola even returned to the States after the war. Still, I'll keep plugging if you think it's worth it. I'll check now for Dimola *in* Imola."

"Yes, and while you're at it look for other Dimolas too," Penny said. "Steven and Inga should have been there at least twice according to my information, but just for the heck of it see if any of the others were aware of Dimola's interest in the village as well. If any of them were up there I'm sure *some* villager would remember—they're a pretty spectacular-looking bunch on the female side. By the way, were the Amalfis blondes?"

"What an extraordinary question! I haven't the faintest idea. What difference does it make?" Toby rumbled.

"Well the Dimola taste runs heavily to blondes. If both Amalfis were blondes he may have dowered them equally with his favors, even if he only married one of them," Penny said coarsely.

"Oh, meaning you think the Contessa's child might have been *his* by-blow? But what difference would that make?"

"It's an idea I've been toying with all along. No *great* difference, I grant you, save in terms of scandal and blackmail, but you might try and get a line on this Lorenzetto— after all he doesn't seem to be around and we've an unaccounted-for body here. Dig some more."

Toby groaned softly to himself. "Well, I'll call you back on what I find in Imola. You making any progress your end?"

"Some. I saw the young Indian today and he helped a bit. And I have hopes of a big breakthrough tomorrow when I talk to Wanda Dimola."

"I only hope you do better than I have so far," Toby said gloomily, and rang off.

He hit pay dirt immediately at the Hotel Olympia in Imola. The hotel clerk was impressed by his official card with its titles, and, after initially demurring for form's sake, dived avidly into the files as a favor to the "milord inglese." Toby silently blessed the requirement for the registration of all foreigners, as he watched the clerk's expert fingers flipping through the cards. He emerged with quite a pile and laid them proudly before Toby. "All we have of the name you requested. I hope you find what you seek. You are welcome to use the desk in the office."

As Toby perused the small stack his eyebrows rose and he became very thoughtful. "Well I'll be jiggered!" he murmured to himself. "It looks as if Penny may have something after all!" There were two entries for Steven Dimola by himself, one with Inga, corresponding to a similar one for Rinaldo. A later one for Rinaldo alone, and, a few days after that, Steven and Inga again. Then a single entry for

Annette Dimola by herself, and two days after that an entry for Alexander and Wanda Dimola. "So they were *all* here sniffing around—but what in Heaven's name *for?*"

Penny retired early from the continuing domestic euphoria in the Langley cottage. She felt unaccountably nervous and badly wanted some time by herself to think about things. First she examined Carson's typewritten account, which was impressively professional. On the local drug scene he had unearthed enough indications, if little actual proof, that Eagle Smith certainly had been one of the suppliers of marijuana and "uppers" for the neighborhood. Among other things, Eagle Smith had made frequent trips to Hyannis to a little novelty store whose proprietor had some very shady connections in Boston and had been under a quiet police scrutiny for some time.

One of the present servants at the Dimola mansion had once been up on a drug charge, when she had become involved in a road accident and some pills had been found in her car. She had been fined and bound over as a first offender. The fine had been paid by Alexander Dimola—which Penny found significant.

Another interesting item had been that several local children, who made it a game to trespass on Zeb's Indian site, knowing full well how furious it made him, had reported that at various times they had seen Inga, Wanda and Steven Dimola alone at the site. (Not that that really meant much, Carson had added in parentheses, all of them got interested in Zeb's work in a casual sort of way and dropped in from time to time to see how he was getting on.)

He had a long paragraph on the mail arrangements of the Dimola estate. Prior to the arrival of the whole family there it had been customary for one of the servants to pick the mail up and distribute it. Since Rinaldo's illness and with so much business mail coming to the house for Alexander, the family had taken over the chore, the only outsider involved in the pickup being Ann.

He had questioned the postmistress at the tiny substation post office, which also handled Western Union for the village, and found that on the day Penny's cable arrived she had got through to the main house but had been unable to contact Zeb direct. She had been told there was something wrong with his line, and, other than that this information came from a woman, she could give no further light on who it was. She had done the next best thing and put the cable in with the morning mail. She was hazy as to who had picked it up that day beyond the fact that "there was a whole carful of them." "Oh dear," Penny murmured in exasperation, "now I suppose I shall have to try and find out who delivered the mail to Zeb that day! How maddening!"

Her nerves were still on the jump, so she slipped quietly into the kitchen to fix herself some warm milk. The children had long gone to sleep—Bobby Grange bedded down on the sofa—but from the hum of conversation from the living room it was evident that the two young parents were still finding plenty to talk about. She felt an awful urge to call Wanda Dimola back, but a glance at her watch showed it was past eleven, no time to place an unobtrusive call to the main house. She resigned herself to the inevitable and settled down to sort out Toby's information.

Apart from the fact that the present Dimola family were the offspring of Rinaldo's second rather than his first marriage, the tragic story of Christiana Amalfi did not seem to have any significance. But how about this Lorenzetto, the child of the lively, worldly sister? Had he been Rinaldo's child? And had Rinaldo on his visit to Colle d'Imola two years previously first become aware of that fact because of the physical resemblance? She frowned. It still did not make any sense.

She could well see that the Contessa Anna-Maria as the woman scorned might have kept the child's real paternity a secret, passing him off as another man's child. She could well see also that Rinaldo, learning of his bastard, might be upset by this blot on the family honor of which he was so proud. Lorenzetto, by Toby's account, was an unsatisfactory character, though he had been unable to clarify this, but if Lorenzetto *were* the body in the bog, why had it taken him two years to appear and put the bite on his famous father?

And again, who of the suspects in the case would be fanatical enough to want to remove him permanently? Annette—who according to her own account thought her husband the most wonderful thing on God's earth? Maria

—who evidently loved her father deeply? His sons—fearful perhaps of the influence of an older half brother? Inga —who was crazy about Steven and would presumably do anything to protect him? Or Zeb—the only one of the whole crowd who was a complete fanatic?

She was back to that again. What if Zeb had been put up to it by one of the Dimolas, who in turn had tried to still his tongue? She sighed wearily and climbed into bed. She was not even sure that any of them knew of Lorenzetto's existence, she would just have to wait for Toby's next report—unless Wanda Dimola could tell her what she wanted to know.

Still absorbed in her problems, she only listened with half an ear to Ann at the breakfast table, as she recounted with some indignation the marital problems Carson Grange had related to her. "His wife sounds like a bitch on wheels! She deserted him and the baby, but now, even though she's shacked up with another man, she's been doing all sorts of things to hurt Carson. She has threatened to try and get Bobby away from him, and she's even tried to break up his relationship with Zeb by telling Zeb a pack of lies about Carson's behavior. It really is too bad! I told him he ought to divorce her, and I think he is starting something now, but he has held off this long because Zeb apparently is very old-fashioned on these lines and persuaded him not to. I think too he was a bit worried about the custody of Bobby."

"Hmm," Penny said abstractedly, "yes, very disturbing." She waited until after Ann had left for work with little Penny, and then hurried over to the Grange house. The large orange cat, whom she had been feeding once a day, was waiting for her on the front porch, his tail lashing furiously. "All right!" she scolded. "I'll feed you! Hold your horses!" She tried the front door and it was locked. "Damn! I thought the house was still open," she muttered. "Maybe the back door is." She hurried around to the back door accompanied by the cat, and was relieved to find that latched but unlocked. She went through the small back hallway into the kitchen, hurriedly opened a can of tuna for the cat and filled a bowl with milk from the refrigerator. She glanced at her watch—it was a few minutes past nine.

She went through the silent house and snubbed back the

Yale lock on the front door, then wandered into the living room to wait. It was so dreary and depressing that she decided she'd wait upstairs in the museum room and quiet her jumping nerves by examining Zeb's collection. The cat, now replete, preceded her up the stairs and accompanied her into the large front room where everything was quiet and orderly. Penny slid back the glass sliding door of the first case and began to look at some Indian cooking pots that Zeb had painstakingly restored. "Not bad," she was musing to herself, when the cat let out a sudden unearthly yowl and, appearing from behind the desk, disappeared out of the door like an orange flash.

Startled herself, Penny looked around to see what had startled the cat. She approached the desk, her ears straining for a noise from below. Then she looked behind it . . .

The small form of Wanda Dimola lay spread-eagled on the floor, hidden from sight by the desk's massive bulk. Her eyes were open and fixed in terror, her fair hair matted with fresh blood. This time there was no doubt about the murder weapon, for by her head lay a large Indian flint pick, its sharp edge blood-stained. Penny looked with sick unbelieving horror at the still figure. For the second time the murderer had struck, and again it was she who had been the unwitting cause . . .

CHAPTER 16

Penny was still in a state of shock, but this time she was determined to bring the two ends of the case together, so she called both the Barnstable and the state police. They arrived almost simultaneously and now Detectives Thompson and Eldredge were listening grim-faced to her account, as the technicians snapped their cameras and dusted the room for prints. Eldredge stood incongruously clutching the murder weapon, which from its very nature would hold no prints. "Reckon the murderer picked up the first thing that came to hand," he said, "and it won't do us one damn bit of good."

"Yes," Penny agreed drearily. "I remember seeing it right there on the desk. I think Zeb must have used it as a paperweight."

"You say you had this appointment for 9 o'clock, that you were only a few minutes late and yet you heard or saw *no one* around?" Detective Thompson glowered at her. "The doctor says she could have died only a few minutes before you got here."

"Yes, for some reason she must have come early. I've no idea why," Penny said, "unless she was looking for something here. But don't you see this points clearly to someone in the Dimola household? *No one* outside knew of my appointment with her. There was only one possible way *anyone* could have known, and that was someone at the house who heard her on the telephone last night and who followed her this morning . . ."

She was interrupted by the door of the museum room bursting open and the insurge of the Dimola family en masse, spearheaded by a white-faced, blazing-eyed Alexander who rushed across the room, brushing aside the small knot of technicians around the body. He knelt down beside it with a little moaning cry and touched the white cheek with a pathetic gentleness, then sprang to his feet, his hate-filled eyes taking in Penny and his brother. "You did it!" he roared at her. "You were responsible, you and your meddling. You got a murderer out of jail and now he has killed her. Damn you to hell!"

He advanced menacingly toward Penny, so that Thompson moved his considerable bulk in front of her. "Now, then, none of that, Mr. Dimola," he said threateningly. "We all know what a shock this is, but calm down, or else . . ."

Even in her own shocked state Penny watched the re-actions of the rest of the Dimolas. It was strange to see the large Inga literally clinging to her smaller husband, her big body shaking uncontrollably, the pale blue, terror-stricken eyes starting out of the pallid face. Steven was the calmest of the group, but there were beads of moisture on his fore-head, and from where she sat she could detect the acrid smell of sweat on him. A nerve jumped under Annette's right eye and she twisted her hands together so tightly that the knuckles stood out white. Maria was biting her lips and shivering, her dark eyes switching from brother to brother as if imploring aid that was not forthcoming.

"Don't you threaten me!" Alexander roared at Thompson. "You've fallen down on your job because of this silly old interfering busybody, but now go get him. I want Eagle Smith—and I won't rest until I see him dead for this."

"Lay off her." A new voice broke in, and Officer Birnie came through the doorway accompanied by Carson Grange. "You're way out of line, Mr. Dimola. Eagle Smith had nothing to do with the murder of your wife." He looked over at his chief. "Acting on information received from State Trooper Grange here, I went over to the Smith cot-tage at 8 o'clock this morning to question Smith concern-ing a possible drug charge. I got him up out of bed. State Trooper Grange joined me at 8:30 and we questioned Smith together until after 9 o'clock. When we came out I heard of the murder here over my car radio. Eagle Smith could not possibly have murdered your wife, Mr. Dimola, he was with us the whole time. But I would very much like to know why *you* think he would have had a strong enough motive to kill her . . ." Again he turned to Detective

Thompson, who was looking startled at this new note of authority from his subordinate. "I think it's high time we started to listen to Dr. Spring here and start treating these three cases as a connected unit." His glance took in Detective Eldredge. "We got nothing out of Eagle Smith on the drug business, but after I'd heard the news I went back into the cottage and told him about the murder. That opened him up. He told me what happened on the bog that day"—Birnie favored Penny with a piercing stare—"and he begged me to find Dr. Spring—he was afraid apparently that someone would try and murder *her*."

Penny was so touched by the young Indian's concern for her safety that had led him to destroy his own, that tears came into her eyes, and Birnie, seeing how the news had affected her, softened his tone. "I'm sorry," he muttered to her, "I didn't want it this way either, but the lad really didn't want you to get hurt." Then collecting himself, he swung around to Alexander Dimola again and snarled, "So I ask you once more, why did you think there was a connection between Eagle Smith and your wife?"

The wild light in Alexander's eye had died out and was replaced by a look of abject misery. "You're sure about this?" It was almost a whisper. Birnie nodded. Alexander's head moved from side to side like an animal in pain. "Oh, what's the use! She's dead, what can it matter to her now!" His voice was agonized. "When I took her to Boston with me this time she went to a doctor. She'd promised me she'd go several times before, but this time I made sure, I went with her. Well, then it all came out. She confessed to the doctor, to me, that she'd been on a steady diet of uppers for over a year, that she was hopelessly hooked on them. I don't know how she made the contact with Smith here—she didn't tell me that—but I do know he *was* her contact. At first she used one of the maids as a go-between. Then, when the maid got picked up, they all got frightened. They'd been using several pick-up points around the estate so as not to arouse anyone's suspicions, the barn on the bog, Zeb's dig, a gardener's shack over by the marsh . . . She swore she wanted to quit and agreed to go into a clinic for a cure . . ." His voice broke a little. "We only came back here for a couple of days to . . . well . . . get together again and sort out what she would need and what we should do about telling the family. I could see she still had something on her mind, but she wouldn't tell me about it. So, when I heard of this, I naturally thought she had tried to buy Smith's silence for the family's sake, but that he'd killed her instead."

"So you knew nothing of her appointment with Dr. Spring?" This from a hard-eyed Detective Thompson.

"No"—Alexander's eyes suddenly blazed into life again as he turned to Penny—"if I had, she would be alive now. I'm sorry for what I said just now, but you were still the cause of her death. So, *do* what you set out to do, find whoever did it. No matter what it costs, how ever long it takes, find the killer. Find out for *me!*"

Before Penny could open her mouth to reply, the two detectives had joined in the chorus. "Yes, Dr. Spring," Thompson said, "perhaps we had better have a conference, if you'd go over the ground again for us." Eldredge agreed.

This time there was an interruption from Carson Grange, who had been silent up to this point. "In the name of humanity, I suggest it be postponed. Anyone with half an eye can see Dr. Spring has had a very severe shock. Look at her, she's as pale as a ghost! Give her some time to recover, for God's sake!"

"But I understand she's been having someone investigate overseas, and we need that information now." Detective Eldredge frowned at his young colleague.

"Can't it wait——" Carson began angrily, but Penny held up a restraining hand.

"It's all right," she said. She summoned up a pale smile for her champion and braced herself to plunge back into the fray. "I'll be glad to give the united police forces what I have so far. It's not a great deal as yet, but I *am* expecting more information very shortly." She paused and let that sink in. "I have nothing that has a direct bearing on *this* tragedy, although one rather interesting fact has come to light. Mr. Rinaldo Dimola was married for the *first* time in Italy during World War II." She stopped and quickly took stock of their reactions. Although the police were looking suitably impressed, the Dimola family greeted her announcement in silence—and she had the feeling that, far from being a shock, it came as no surprise to any of them . . .

Toby returned to Colle d'Imola with the distinct feeling he had at last accomplished something useful to pass on to Penny, even if he was not quite sure what that accomplishment was.

He shied away from thinking about his next target, the reclusive Contessa. From what little he had heard she sounded the very last kind of woman that he would ever seek out of his own accord. Indeed, the very thought of her frightened him half to death, but it was something that just had to be done. He sighed inwardly. The only means of entrée would have to be the priest. This thought cheered him slightly, because what could possibly happen with a priest around? However, the priest would have to be approached with a great deal of tact, for he would not appreciate the fact that Toby's object was to rattle the skeletons in the family closet of his most prestigious parishioner.

How to go about it? This question absorbed him as he absentmindedly ate his way through the substantial dinner provided by Mrs. Enrico. After it, he did not join the group in the bar, but sat in gloomy state in the parlor, puffing furiously on his pipe until the whole room was enveloped in an aromatic blue cloud, and aiding his cogitations by liberal libations from the bottle of a rare rosé Enrico had triumphantly produced for him.

As it turned out he could have saved himself the effort; the priest came looking for him. An obviously impressed Mrs. Enrico came rapping at the door to say Padre Antonio was outside and would like to speak with the Signore. Quickly recovering from his own surprise, Toby rumbled a mellifluous assent, and as an afterthought asked her to bring another glass for his unexpected visitor. With a despairing glance at her white lace curtains, already yellowing under the assault of Toby's tobacco fumes, Mrs. Enrico hurried off as bidden and returned with both priest and glass.

The priest was a palely plump man of young middle age, with a great deal of lank black hair and a tendency to sweat. His black soutane was shiny with long wear, and by the hungry way he eyed the wine bottle Toby deduced that this parish priest at least was not one who enjoyed the fat of the land.

"Sir Glendower, it is indeed a pleasure to welcome a person of such eminence to our village," he said, proferring a wet, plump hand.

"Professor Glendower," Toby corrected, for he privately loathed his title and only used it under extreme duress.

"Oh, *professore!*" The priest's face fell a little. "I had understood that you bore a title."

"Well I do," Toby agreed grumpily, "but I don't use it much, but *if* used it should be Sir Tobias."

The priest looked totally confused, and Toby was glad to see that he seemed as nervous as he was himself.

He offered a glass of wine, which was accepted with alacrity, and the priest, perched on the edge of one of the hideous magenta armchairs, took several grateful sips before reopening the conversation. "I understand you are here on business," he said tentatively. "Perhaps I may be of some service to you."

Toby nodded. "Perhaps."

"A professore of history? This has been a most interesting area; I can tell you much of it."

"No, I'm a professor of archaeology."

The priest looked further confused. "Oh, I'm afraid I know little of that. There is not much here that I know of. Is there something in particular you are seeking?"

Toby relented a little. "Actually I am concerned here with fairly recent history. I am making enquiries for a friend about a man who was here in the war and was also back here about two years ago." He carefully replenished the priest's glass, which finished the bottle, and stood up. "I think I will ask Enrico if he can find us another bottle of this excellent vintage," he said, and watched Father Antonio narrowly as he went on: "The name of the man was Rinaldo Dimola—I hope you can tell me something of him." He went quietly out, leaving the priest looking thoughtfully at the deep pink liquid in his glass, and as Toby collected another bottle from Enrico he was positive that the name had indeed hit home.

When he returned the priest was expressionless, but there were little beads of sweat on his brow. "I was not here during the war. I am not from this region," he said, "I am from Verona, so I am afraid I can be of little help."

"But you were here two years ago," Toby persisted. "Did you see him then? He was here on several occasions."

"Yes, I believe so," Father Antonio admitted with considerable reluctance. "I met him in the churchyard—he was putting flowers on a grave there."

"Yes, the memorial of his wife, Christiana Amalfi," Toby said with deliberation.

The priest looked thunderstruck. "His wife!"

"Yes. They were married right here in Colle d'Imola. It is strange that she was buried under her maiden name, is it not?"

"Indeed!" the priest muttered, and avoided his eyes.

"Did you notice any other strangers equally interested in your churchyard about that time?"

"Why yes!" Father Antonio seemed to welcome this change of subject. "There were several American ladies, very lovely, blonde American ladies. One gave me a donation for the church."

"How many of them?"

"Two—no, three, I think."

"Any men?"

The priest used the same line as Enrico. "In summer we often get tourist—one cannot keep track." His brow clouded. "But there was one young man who was like the man of whom you speak. He could have been a son. You are acting for this man?"

It was a strange way of putting it. "No," Toby said truthfully, "but Rinaldo Dimola is a man of great importance and lies stricken, unable to speak for himself. We are trying to elucidate an important matter that has come up concerning him."

"I am sorry to hear that," the priest muttered automatically. "You say 'we'—you have a companion here?" He sounded anxious.

Again that seemed an odd remark to Toby. "No—she is in America, on the Dimola estate." A small silence ensued.

Toby decided it was time to take the bull by the horns. "It would be of considerable help to me if I could speak with the Contessa," he said with deliberation. "I understand that you are the only person in the village who visits the palazzo. Would it be possible to ask her to grant me an interview?"

To his amazement the priest gave him a sudden beaming smile. "Why, how fortunate you should say that! I came tonight not only to make your acquaintance, professore, but also, I confess, in the role of emissary. The Contessa, you understand, rarely has the pleasure of talking with anyone of her own social standing. She was much excited when she heard that a milord inglese was staying in the village and asked me if I would seek you out and invite you to the palazzo."

Toby was suitably startled. "I would be most happy indeed to go with you to see the Contessa," he said a little anxiously. "When would it be convenient?"

The priest was now positively animated. "Why not tomorrow morning, say around 11—the Contessa is a late riser. I will come for you here."

"Excellent!" Toby, elated by this, went to pour the priest another glass, but Father Antonio shook his head and got to his feet. The animation died out of his face. "It grows late, professore, and I must say early Mass tomorrow. There is one thing I must tell you before you go to the palazzo." His dark eyes were troubled. "The Contessa is a very sick woman, sicker than she knows. And she is very greatly troubled in her mind about her son. I must not cast stones, Sir Tobias, but he has always been a great burden to her. Nevertheless, she loves him dearly—and now, it seems, he has disappeared."

CHAPTER 17

Despite the lateness of the hour, Toby put in a call to Penny, whom he caught just about to sit down to an insubstantial dinner. He was so elated by his own progress that he rattled on, oblivious to a certain lack of response from his partner. "So it really looks as if you are on to something," he concluded. "The Contessa's unsatisfactory son is missing and *all* your suspects were sniffing around here on the heels of Rinaldo two years ago. I could not find any trace of Steven in *Colle* d'Imola but all the rest were seen by the priest."

"Steven isn't very noticeable, so he may have been there too." Penny's voice sounded very weary. "And you can scratch one of my former suspects—she was murdered this morning." Rapidly she filled him in on the latest catastrophe and he listened in worried silence. At the end he said, "Are you all right? You sound terrible. I wish to Heaven you'd get out of there, go to Boston or something. I don't like the way things are going one little bit."

"Oh, Toby, how *can* I? I admit this has hit me pretty hard, but I feel responsible for that poor girl's death. I *have* to see it through now. The worst of it is that I think this was probably an unnecessary murder—the murderer must be starting to panic. I have the awful hunch that all poor Wanda was about to do was to confess to me about the drug business in an effort to get Eagle Smith off the hook on the more serious charge. The devil of it is I can't be sure. However, the murderer may have gone too far this time—both police forces are now working on the case, and pure routine investigation may pin down which of the Dimolas could have been at the Grange house at that early hour. But what still puzzles me about your end of it is why it took Lorenzetto—*if* he is the body in the bog—two years to do anything about his father. If you can turn up anything on that it would be a great help."

139

"Well, as I said, I'm off to see the Contessa in the morning," Toby said, with a great deal more confidence than he felt. "And I'll get in touch with you as soon as I can after. And, for God's sake, Penny, be *careful*."

"I will, my dear," she soothed, "and thanks for the information—it will help to keep my policemen happy; they are beginning to look on me as something of a Jonah."

The next morning Toby spruced himself up bright and early and, as the hour of 11 approached, fortified himself with a shot or two of local brandy, which proved to be terrible. Father Antonio appeared promptly and solemnly escorted him across the square to the peeling, closed doors of the palazzo, letting them in through the small wicket gate that was embedded in one of the larger doors.

Through the cavernous, echoing entranceway they made their way into the courtyard, which spoke in mute eloquence of the palazzo's ruinous state; blocks of masonry and pieces of decorated cornice lay haphazardly around, with the gaunt skeletons of last year's wild flowers and weeds growing up in between them. Many of the windows that overlooked the courtyard were cracked or the glass gone entirely, and long green stains ran down the honey-colored inner walls like spreading blight from the choked and ruptured gutters and drainpipes. Father Antonio led the way through this maze of decay to a area in the back of the palazzo that looked a little less ruinous than the rest. "The palace was much damaged in the war," he apologized, "and since, I fear, there has not been the money to do anything about it. The Contessa has a suite in the garden wing at the back here." He threw open another large door on a completely empty hallway, which ran through the breadth of the wing to dusty, glass French doors at the opposite end; weak sunlight filtered through them and made faint patterns on the black-and-white tiled floor, and beyond, Toby could see the garden in riotous ruin of vegetation. A grand marble stairway reared itself upward to the shadows, and on the walls could be seen faint marks where large pictures had long since been removed.

The priest opened a gilded door to the left and called out, "Contessa, it is I with the milord inglese. May we

come in?" A faint voice answered and he beckoned Toby
to enter.

They went into a large, cluttered room full of patched
or broken antique furniture. The Contessa was seated in
a high-backed armchair, one of the few seemingly intact
articles of furniture in the place; there was a small table
at her side with a dusty carafe of wine and two glasses
on it.

She did not rise to greet them, but extended a hand to
Toby as he was led up and introduced by Father Antonio.
Feeling acutely uncomfortable, he took the hand and bowed
over it stiffly. A pair of brilliant dark eyes swept up at him
out of a ravaged face. Though the Contessa had applied
a lot of makeup there was no disguising the grayish tone
of the skin or the lines that pain and dissipation had left
upon it. Even the jet-black hair was streaked with white,
which Toby knew to be unusual for an Italian. She waved
him graciously to a seat and he perched his lanky frame
gingerly on a frail-looking love seat. "I hope you will take
a glass of wine with me, Sir Tobias, to celebrate your visit,"
she murmured in the sweet melodious Italian which has
been the hallmark of the Imolese since the time of Dante.
Toby, who was no slouch when it came to honeyed accents,
rumbled an equally melodious assent. "You may serve us,
Padre, and then you may leave us—I would like to be alone
with Sir Tobias," she ordered. The two men stared at her
in surprise, Toby frankly aghast. The priest meekly did
as he was bidden and then almost backed out of the room,
muttering vague farewells.

The dark eyes sparkled at Toby coquettishly over the
rim of her glass as she sipped. "So we are alone, Sir Toby,"
she purred. "Now we can really talk."

"Er, yes," Toby stammered.

"I am told you are here on business." Her tone became
crisper and harder. "Did *he* send you?"

"He? Who?"

"Why the great Rinaldo Dimola, of course—who else?"
There was venom in her voice.

"No he didn't"—Toby met her hard bold stare with innocent round blue eyes—"but I gather you do not care for
him very much."

"I hate him and everything about him," she hissed, "for what he has done to me and mine."

"For marrying your sister, do you mean?" Toby said with continued innocence.

She was silent for a moment and her eyes narrowed. "So you know about that."

"Yes. I also know he was here two years ago. You saw him then, didn't you?"

"If you are not from him or his brood, how do you know so much about him and his movements?" Her tone was suspicious.

"I am investigating for a friend." Toby was treading very carefully. "Business connected with a friend of hers which she feels has its roots in the visit Dimola paid here two years ago."

"So you are an investigator. How odd!" It was almost a sneer, but again the coquettish note crept into her voice. "Perhaps then you could investigate something for me." Her tone sharpened and there was both fear and hope in it. "This friend of yours is not by any chance a friend of Lorenzo's?"

"Lorenzo?" Toby was puzzled.

She made a little impatient gesture with her hand. "Lorenzo—my son."

"Oh. I had understood he was, er, called Lorenzetto."

She gestured again. "Oh, that is what the villagers have always called him, to distinguish him from my Lorenzo, my husband." The dark eyes challenged.

"Ah, I see, from his father," Toby said primly. "No, my friend knows nothing of him."

She said nothing but stared unblinkingly at him.

"As I said," he went on, "I am deeply involved with my friend's business, but if there is anything I can do for you in connection with your son I should be happy to try, particularly if you can give me any assistance on Dimola's visit here. Rinaldo *did* come to the palazzo, didn't he?"

"Oh, yes, he was here"—she gave a scornful laugh—"the great successful millionaire was here. How he must have enjoyed seeing me like this!" She made an angry gesture at the ruin around her. "And that fool of a maid

I had then letting him in——" She checked herself suddenly, as if she had said too much.

"And what is the nature of your problem with Lorenzo?" Toby asked patiently.

"Always so thoughtless—the *wretched* boy!" She tried to achieve lightness but failed miserably. "Not a *line* from him in months. I don't know *where* he's got to!"

"So you'd like me to try and find him? I could certainly try. Do you have a recent picture of him? I would need that." Toby tried not to sound eager. "Or identifying marks —had he any broken bones or anything distinctive?"

Again she stared at him searchingly. "Why do you ask that? Do you swear on your honor you are not working for Rinaldo?"

"I do indeed. I have never encountered either him or his family in any way, nor probably will I ever," Toby assured her.

Her eyes still fixed on his, her hand went toward a small drawer in the table by her side; she opened it and withdrew a picture in a tarnished silver frame. Silently she offered it to Toby. The somber-faced young man in it was short and of but medium build, but there was no mistaking the face —it was the face of Rinaldo Dimola. Toby said nothing, but withdrew the teleprinted photo from his inside pocket and put the picture of the young soldier by the side of Lorenzo's and handed them to her. "So that was it?" he said. "And Rinaldo never knew until he came back here two years ago?"

"No, damn him to hell!" There was a savage glee about her. "My one, my only, triumph over him—and he never would have known about Lorenzo if that fool of a maid had not let him in here before I got to this." She clutched the framed photo to her breast. "Not that it did him much good—I saw to that! I wouldn't tell him where Lorenzo was, only that he had gone away and that he would never see his son—never!"

Suddenly her face crumpled and she cried out, "Oh, for God's sake help me! Get Lorenzo back! I don't know how Rinaldo did it, but somehow the demon must have found him. I don't see *how*, he wasn't even using his own name——" She broke off and a great sob welled up, shaking the emaciated frame. "But I'm *sure* Rinaldo did find him. When Lorenzo was here eight months ago he was up to something—oh, how well I know it!—a demon just like his father! And not a word from him since." She rose, and to Toby's horror came over to him and sank to her knees, grasping at his hands with her own feverish ones. "I'm not such a fool as they think I am. I know I haven't long to live. Afterwards Rinaldo can have him—that's what Lorenzo will be after, the money, the power, because there is no love in him, none—they'll deserve one another. But get him back for me now! He's all I have, all I've ever had. It will only be for a little while. But get Rinaldo to let me have him back, if there is any mercy at all in his heart . . ."

Toby, although he was overwhelmed with pity for her, was reduced to stuttering embarrassment. "Contessa, you must realize that Rinaldo has no claim on him, or he on Rinaldo. He is *yours*." He was as certain now as Penny was that Lorenzo was long past any human claims on him, but he knew this was no time to break such news to the dying woman before him; now was the time for comfort.

She drew back from him and a mocking light came into her eyes. She got up and resumed her seat in the high-backed chair. "So you don't understand," she said dully, "any more than anyone else has ever understood. How could they since it is something only Rinaldo and I would and *could* know. Lorenzo is Rinaldo's son, but he isn't mine—he is Christiana's."

"Good God!" said Toby.

Penny returned from an early morning conference with the police in a somewhat dazed state, stemming from all the detailed reports they had hurled at her. She felt disinclined for some reason to go back to the Langley cottage, and instead made her way through the pale spring sunshine to the porch of the Grange house, where her friend and fellow body finder, the orange cat, was awaiting her. She fed him absentmindedly and then went to sit on the steps of the front porch in the sun to try and sort things out.

No dramatic discovery had been made. The police had interviewed all the servants and all the Dimolas about their whereabouts at the time of Wanda's murder; most of the servants had solid alibis, being in one another's sight at some time in the vital period, but the stories of the Dimolas were more nebulous and, while seemingly perfectly innocent and understandable, were almost impossible to prove or disprove. One of them was lying—but which?

Annette, who since her husband's illness had occupied a separate room, had, according to her, slept late and had not risen until about 9 o'clock. No one had seen her before that.

Inga had taken over from one of the servants who kept the night watch on Rinaldo at 8 o'clock and claimed she had been in the sick room the whole time. No one had seen her.

Maria said that she and Inga had parted after breakfasting together and that she had gone for a walk on the marsh alone. Again, no one had seen her.

Steven had been late to breakfast, had stated he had risen at 7:30 and then had put in some time in his study on notes he had wanted to finish before eating breakfast. A servant had seen him coming out of his study at some time after 9, but, since the study had a sliding glass door opening on the seaward terrace, he could have entered and exited by it without anyone being the wiser.

Alexander's account had been the most interesting. According to him, he and Wanda had got up together at 7:30. This was unusual for her, but he had thought it part of their newfound "togetherness." She had showered first, and by the time he had showered and shaved she had gone from their room. He had assumed she had breakfast in the morning room but, not finding her there, had thought she had skipped it as she often did, and after grabbing a hasty cup of coffee himself (seen by a servant) had gone up to his father's study and had worked on business papers there until the call from the police had arrived. A servant had seen him going into the study but could not be pinned down as to the time; Alexander claimed that it was around 8:30.

The police were much concerned as to how Wanda and her murderer had come to the Grange house. There were no fresh tire tracks in the wet earth of the glade, no evidence that any of the Dimola cars had been used that morning. Wanda had had on walking shoes on which sand

and pine needles had been found and, while the detective who did the lab examinations would not commit himself before he had examined his finds under a microscope, he had expressed the opinion that some of the sand was beach sand, so at some point Wanda had walked along a beach on her journey to her ill-fated rendezvous.

That's something to check on, Penny thought, I must find how she came. If she did come on the sand, maybe there'll be traces of whoever followed her as well. She got up and looked around to get her bearings. It would be in the opposite direction from the bog, that was certain. She crossed over to the other side of the glade and searched around; there seemed a myriad of little footpaths leading off on that side, but the one farthest to the left, she reasoned, should be the one most nearly adjacent to the beach.

She started along the thick carpet of pine needles, searching the ground carefully; the path kept veering to the left, and in one sandy patch she suddenly spotted something—it was the track of a bicycle wheel. With mounting excitement she traced it as the sandy patches became more frequent as she neared the beach. Rounding a corner suddenly she let out a little yelp of fright as a figure loomed on the path ahead.

"Good morning, Dr. Spring," Officer Birnie said with a faint smile, "I see we're on the same track today," and chortled at his own joke.

"You've followed the bicycle from the house?" she asked eagerly. "I don't see how it could have got off the isthmus the house stands on without going through the main gate."

He jerked his head back over his shoulder. "There's a footbridge from the house over the inlet just inside the fence. I've followed the track from there, and there's a shed full of bicycles some distance from the house. The tracks go to the glade?"

She nodded. "I thought so," he said. "Well, now we know how the murderer got there."

"How do you know it wasn't Wanda? The murderer could have taken the bike away with him."

He shook his head. "No, I'm pretty sure I've found where she walked on the beach away from the house and then cut back into the pines. Come, I'll show you." He led the way until they got in sight of the footbridge spanning the small tidal creek. Then he stopped and looked curiously at her. "By the way," he said, "there's something I haven't put in any report yet, but it's a bit of information which I think it would be safer for you to know. You know I said I went to Eagle Smith's at 8? Well, Carson Grange was supposed to be there to meet me. He didn't turn up until 8:30. He'd have had time, you know."

Penny looked at him with a worried frown. "But that wouldn't make any sense in view of all the rest of it—he would have no possible motive."

He stared out across the gray-green tumbling waters of the bay. "People can be bought, you know," he said heavily, "especially when money is no object to the buyers."

CHAPTER 18

She got back to the Langley cottage to find a state police car parked in front of it and a young trooper she had not seen before leaning on the hood and smoking a quiet cigarette. He dropped it hastily at the sight of her and said with some relief, "Dr. Spring? We've been looking all over for you. A Professor Glendower called us from Italy; seems he has been trying to contact you all morning with important information, and he's worried about you. Could you call him right away?"

Penny glanced doubtfully at the cottage. She really did not want any long-distance call going through the main house exchange at this juncture, and her heart failed at the thought of trying to get through at the booth at Chase's Variety Store. "Could I make the call from your station?" she asked. "I'll gladly pay."

"It'll mean going clean over to South Yarmouth," he said reluctantly. "Why not call from here?"

"Young man, there is a killer up at the mansion *and* a listening post at the exchange there," Penny said severely. "I very much doubt whether Detective Eldredge would want me to make a call from here any more than I'd want to."

"Oh, all right," he agreed, and drove them in gloomy silence the fair distance to the state police post in South Yarmouth. There the gods were with her and in a very short time she was connected with Toby, who was literally hanging by the phone at his end in a state of acute anxiety.

"You all in one piece?" he enquired immediately, and on being assured she was he continued in an aggrieved fashion. "Well, while sniffing around after the murderer you might at least have given a *thought* to me. You knew I was going to see the Contessa."

She soothed and apologized and he rumbled on excitedly about the amazing fruits of his labors. She listened in growing amazement. "End-so, and-so, la-la-la," she said suddenly. "So that was what he was trying to say!"

"What on earth are you babbling about?" Toby, halted in mid-sentence, said vexedly.

"Rinaldo! He was trying to say 'Lorenzo,' and presumably 'Anna' or 'Christiana' too. Oh, I'll explain later! Go on!"

Then as he got to the end of his narrative she said, "Yes, I see that clears it all up, barring one fact—*why* did it take Lorenzo so long to get here?"

"I still don't know that. I'd been doing fine and then rather blew it at the end. *I* was upset to see her so upset, so I let slip that Rinaldo had had this stroke and was out of action. When she heard that she just went off into peals of laughter. I thought she'd never stop—it was ghastly! Talk about 'Hell hath no fury like a woman scorned'! After that she shut up entirely. Either she didn't know or wouldn't say. But before that I had got a couple of interesting facts out of her. Number one was that Lorenzo did suffer a broken wrist falling from a horse when he was thirteen, and second, he did not always use the name of Amalfi, he sometimes used Salas, apparently the partisan leader's name, and sometimes Lucca, which indicates to me that perhaps he was mixed up in crooked business of some kind and *may* have a record. Anyway, this should give the police at your end something to go on. He may have had a passport under one or other of the names so they should be able to track down his port of entry. It would be between eight months ago when his mother—or rather, his aunt—last saw him and six months ago when presumably he was murdered. So that should give them a narrow time period to work with and I may be able to pin it down still more."

"Fingerprints," Penny said abruptly. She looked at Detective Eldredge who had been hovering nearby looking hopeful. "You got them from the body, didn't you?" He nodded.

"Then tell the Italian police a set of the dead man's prints will be on the way," she told Toby. "It's possible he had a record and that will cinch the matter of identity. How soon?" She cocked an eye at Eldredge.

"Right away. If I send them off now, they'll get 'em

in Rome late tonight or early tomorrow." There was the gleam of battle in his eye.

"O.K., Toby, I'll get back to you soon—you're a miracle worker," Penny encouraged, and cradled the phone.

"Well, what was that all about?" Eldredge demanded. She told him. At the end of it he looked at her with grudging admiration. "Seems I owe you an apology. You were on the right track all along. A legitimate son by a previous marriage, eh? Ee-yah, that'll put an almighty flutter in the Dimola dovecote, particularly if the old man kicks off, I reckon." He said it with relish.

"Quite," Penny said frostily. "So, if you'll excuse me now, Detective Eldredge, I have a lot of thinking to do."

"Oh, no need to worry yourself any more." He was cheerful. "We can handle it all now. Just relax and let us handle it from here on in." He might have saved his breath, as Toby could well have told him. The gleam of battle in her own eye, Penny smiled at him vaguely and said, "Well, thank you. Would you mind having someone take me back now?"

"Why certainly, certainly," he said with evident relief at his easy victory, "and I'll be sure and let you know how things turn out on this Lorenzo Amalfi or Dimola."

Over the faint and fruitless protestations of her driver, she detoured by the police station in Hyannis and, asking for Detective Thompson, got instead Officer Birnie, which suited her well enough. She quickly filled him in on what she had just told the state police and concluded with, "I haven't thought it through yet, but I believe we're going to find it narrows the field considerably. However, until we know something concrete on Lorenzo's movements I feel it might be wise to put a police guard on Zeb."

He shook his head at her in reproof. "We're way ahead of you, Dr. Spring—half an hour after we got the news of Wanda Dimola's murder there was a policeman at the door of his room, who won't be removed until after we have the murderer in custody."

She laughed. "I'm sorry. What an old busybody you must think me! Have any of the family tried to see him?"

He smiled back at her. "The whole damn lot at one time or another. Mightily concerned about Zeb Grange they are—including Carson."

"At least that's understandable," Penny said defensively.

"Oh, yes—highly," he said, and the smile died. "I don't suppose you'd consider going up to Boston for a few days until we see our way a bit clearer?"

She shook her head. "I was afraid you wouldn't," he gloomed. "Oh, well, just be careful, we're stretched so thin we can't spare a man to keep an eye on *you*."

She rejoined her restive state trooper and drove back to the cottage, going directly to her room, where she perched on the edge of the bed, cleared off the bedside table, and got busy with pen and paper to aid her thoughts.

Two years ago Rinaldo Dimola, on a nostalgic visit to the scene of his first brief love with Christiana Amalfi, had stumbled by chance on the secret the rejected Anna-Maria Amalfi had kept so long and so vengefully—he had a legitimate son, the image of himself, whom he had never seen. His *eldest* son. To a man with Rinaldo's sense of family honor what a cataclysmic revelation that must have been. No wonder his character had changed after that. But *why* had he kept it to himself and *why* had it taken Lorenzo so long to get to his father?

Did any of the others know? She could not understand how any of them could have known the whole story, since only Rinaldo and the Contessa had known that. But they had all been sniffing around after Rinaldo—even the enigmatic Annette, who, according to her own account, had not been to Colle d'Imola at all. They must have suspected something, and one or more of them had been sufficiently alarmed to keep a close enough eye on Rinaldo to intercept and remove the interloper before he ever came under his father's roof.

At least, she comforted herself, now there would be a lot of leads to follow up. Rinaldo, after that soul-shattering discovery he had an unknown legitimate son, must have instituted a search for him. Private detective agencies both here and in Italy could be canvassed, even if Toby failed to turn up any further concrete information as to where the missing Lorenzo was all that time. Would anyone have known about that search? Alexander possibly, since he was so intimately concerned with his father's business affairs. What had Maria said about that? that her father had looked at Alexander with pity! Pity because the hierarchy of the

Dimola family was going to be drastically changed? Or pity because he knew that Alexander shared part of his awful knowledge?

But something about this irked her. Lorenzo's killer, Zeb's attacker and Wanda's murderer must on the face of it be one and the same person. And she just could not see Alexander coldbloodedly striking down his wife and then putting on an act such as she had witnessed in Zeb's house. He had been grief-stricken and angry, and, unless he was the world's greatest actor, she would have sworn those emotions were genuine. No, she felt she was getting off the track.

Back to Rinaldo. He must have had some sort of plan for introducing the missing heir to his second family. It was pure guesswork now, but had Lorenzo jumped the gun on this plan, notified his father he was on his way, and was *this* the shock that brought on Rinaldo's stroke? He had been found in his study slumped over his desk—so something in the mail that day? It was another thing to be checked.

His impaired mind had kept on hoping—she well remembered that terrible gleam of hope when Maria had announced, "a stranger to see you." Yet something Maria had told him about the inquest upset him so badly that he must have known at that point that his eldest son was, in fact, the body in the bog—and that someone close to him had brought this about. She thought of the terrible finality of that "No" to Maria. Rinaldo knew—or thought he knew —who that person was and, if Penny were any judge of character, would carry that secret to his grave. She sighed wearily—she was getting nowhere.

Attack it from another angle. Back to Zeb. Zeb had investigated that disturbed grave and found the body— and had seen lying there the living image of his idol Rinaldo. He had panicked, and in his loyalty and innate secrecy had initiated the weird series of events that had brought her into the case.

But the murderer had been ahead of him, removing the body and mutilating it so that later identification would be impossible. And, save for the unfortunate perspicacity of young Robert Dyke, would have probably succeeded. The murderer knew he could rely on the silence of the eccentric

Zeb as long as his idol's secret was involved, and so long as he had no tangible evidence for his basic honesty to work on. With the finding of the body again the danger had returned: Zeb's turning to her and about to pass on the one vital fact that would uncover the body's identity—the likeness. The killer had started to panic then. It had been stupid to remove that photo, the one *smiling* photo extant of Rinaldo that had given her her first idea about the case. The panic had continued in that the murderer had not completed Zeb's quietus due to the fortuitous advent of Eagle Smith on his own illicit errands, and had been living ever since on a razor's edge of fear lest Zeb came out of his coma before he died and told . . . But was the fear justified? Zeb was going to tell her but not the police. Would his fanatic loyalty still keep him silent? It would not surprise her; if Rinaldo was not talking, she had the feeling neither would Zeb. This too seemed to be leading to a dead end, and there was still no clear picture of the murderer.

Another angle. Motive. Suddenly her mind seemed to clear and for the first time a straighter path appeared before her. Her notes became more decisive.

Annette Dimola: apparently devoted to her husband; involved at one time with Steven; something of a liar; but to whom Lorenzo's advent might have been uncomfortable though little more. *Her* position would in no way be threatened, nor her life with Rinaldo. She was inclined to rule out Annette.

Maria; again, fonder of her father than anyone dreamed of or understood; an ardent women's libber who felt unfairly done in by her father's superpatriarchal household. The advent of a third brother would be a further blow to her feminist ego, but that scarcely would be a strong enough motive to involve her in the cold-blooded murder of a man she had never seen. Also Penny seriously doubted she would have had the physical strength to carry out all the murderer had had to do; she was small and not particularly muscular. So Maria was ruled out.

Alexander: the motive here was stronger undoubtedly; from younger son to youngest, *but* he was still his father's right hand and like him in all ways. Even with the unknown and, according to all accounts so far, the unsatisfactory Lorenzo's advent, she simply could not see Rinaldo taking the business out of Alexander's control; Rinaldo was fanatical in some ways but he certainly wasn't stupid. And she also could not see Alexander murdering his own wife, who, though she had been a problem, he had evidently deeply loved. So Alexander was out.

Which brought her to the pair who, without a shadow of doubt, had the most powerful motive of all. Steven, the quiet, passive, scholarly Steven, with none of his younger brother's dynamism, but basking nonetheless in his father's approval because he was the *elder,* the heir, as he thought, and who stood to lose all of that. Steven, besides, with the tough, enduring genes of his mother's New England blood, that clung to what it had and did not give it up. Steven, the pampered and the vain, who evidently liked the fuss his possessive wife made over him and equally enjoyed the devotion—possibly the love?—of his glamorous assistant Ann Langley. Vanity was so often a part of a murderer's makeup, allowing them the God-like feeling that life was theirs to dispose of, stifling conscience, nullifying fear. And also Steven the scholarly researcher who just *might* have stumbled on the truth in that faraway Italian village and had lain in patient wait.

And his Valkyrie wife, Inga. She, who was so shrewd in some ways, so opaque in others, yet single-minded and domineering. Greedy, jealous of the good things her rich alliance had brought her. Obsessed by her husband, who would be displaced by the interloper, and she too reduced from wife of the heir to just another Dimola woman. Inga, the health freak, with the physical strength and ability to take care of the threats to her comfortable existence.

One or both of them. It would explain so much. Rinaldo's refusal to speak—for if it were Steven he would never give up his son, even for the crime of fratricide. Or even if Inga had *told* him it was Steven, the effect would be the same. The more Penny thought about it the more sense it made. Inga with the upper hand in the sick room; the slow recovery, or lack of it, of Rinaldo, the only progress made after *Maria* had insisted on bringing in a new doctor, Inga's heavy sedation of her helpless patient in recent weeks. If Rinaldo died now, nothing would keep Steven from his inheritance—only a charge of murder. But how could it ever be brought home to them?

The police would presumably find Lorenzo's trail to Masuit eventually, but then what? How to prove who had lured Lorenzo to the excavation site on God knows what pretext and there murdered him? Zeb's attack. With Zeb's lips sealed by his loyalty to Rinaldo, what hope there? None, she thought. And with the murder of Wanda? At the time of the crime Steven said he had been in his study, but could easily have got out and slipped away unseen. Inga had claimed to be in the sickroom, but who was to say she had *not* been? Rinaldo, if he were conscious? Never in a million years.

"There must be *some* way to do it," Penny said aloud, "some to make them show their hand." One or both—the more she thought about it the more she favored just one—but how to prove it? A slow smile spread across the ugly little face. "I believe that would work! At least it would be worth a try. But I mustn't be stupid about this, I'll need help to set it up."

As if in answer to the thought a voice called from the lounge, "Anybody home?" She opened her door to see Carson Grange, his son firmly by the hand, young Penny straddling his shoulders, standing in the middle of the room. "Ann around?" he enquired cheerfully. "I picked up Penny for her. I thought we might take them to McDonald's for a bite." The children made enthusiastic, affirmative noises.

Penny looked steadily at him for a moment. Despite all Officer Birnie's misgivings, she could not find it in her heart to doubt Carson or his motives. "Yes, Ann will be in soon," she said, "but I've been doing some heavy thinking. I have a plan, and I'll need your help on it. Can you park the children somewhere and come in for a minute? You see this is what I've got in mind . . ."

CHAPTER 19

Toby was feeling goaded. There had been a point in the Pergama case when he had been seized by this terrible feeling of urgency, a sort of inner boiling that would allow him no rest; and now this feeling was back, and he did not like it one little bit.

The immediate thing was to find out where Lorenzo had been during that strange hiatus, and what he had been up to. What sort of person had he been, in fact? Everyone, including his putative mother, had so far not had a good word to say about him, but Toby still had no concrete idea as to why they had all thought him so awful. He shied away from the thought of another confrontation with the Contessa, and that only seemed to leave him with one alternative, Father Antonio. He sought him out at the shabby little presbytery adjacent to the new church, at a slight remove from the village.

His new anxiety put sternness into his normally cherubic features and straightened his frame from its exaggerated scholar's stoop, so that he made an intimidating picture to the priest, who opened the door to the presbytery himself. "Matters have become grave and urgent," Toby trumpeted to the startled man. "I have sad news to give you and there is information which it is vital you should give me in return."

He was ushered into the bleak room that evidently served the double purpose of study and refectory. When they were both seated the priest cleared his throat nervously. "In what way can I help you, professore?"

"It is to do with the missing Lorenzo Amalfi," stated Toby, his anxiety making him brusque. "After seeing the Contessa I am in accord with your view that she is a very sick woman, whose time is rapidly running out. You seem to be her only close contact, so I feel I must leave it up to you either to tell her or to prepare her for the sad news. There seems little doubt that Lorenzo Amalfi is dead—murdered, and that he was killed over six months ago on his father's estate in America. His murderer has killed again and is still being sought, and so it is *vital* that you tell me everything you know about him and his activities."

The little priest looked aghast. "You are sure of this?"

"Almost certain," Toby answered. "The anatomical description of the body fits that of Amalfi exactly and his fingerprints are on the way to the Italian police, which should clinch the matter—from his army record here if nowhere else."

The priest made a helpless little fluttering gesture with his hands. "Then if the fingerprints are his, the police will know. Alas! Lorenzo was well known to them, he has quite a record. It has been a great grief to his mother, a great grief, poor woman."

"Then please tell me all about it."

The little man became agitated. "You must understand, Sir Glendower, I do not know much of his early life. I came to the village just fifteen years ago when he was already grown and the pattern started. I can only tell you what I have heard. In many ways he was unfortunate. The Contessa, well, one must not judge . . . but her way of life . . . and then how she treated him; spoiling him one minute, rejecting him the next. It was not easy for him, no!"

"Oh, get on with it, man!" Toby said testily.

The priest gulped and went on. "As a child, I believe, he was very isolated—the Contessa did not let him mix with the villagers and he was a little terror to them. He was always so full of bottled-up energy; a kind of dynamism that was trying to get out but could not find a channel. There was still some money then, and when the Contessa, er, had a companion, he was often shipped off to a boarding school. But there would be trouble at the school or the man would go, and then he would be brought back and it would start all over again between them. The school scrapes were all minor ones, you understand, and things didn't get serious until he was about eighteen. It was then he assaulted a man who was living at the palazzo and took the man's car and drove it off a cliff. He was always mad about cars . . ." The priest gave a little sigh and shook his head. "The man brought charges and though the Contessa managed to hush things up, well, from then on the police had their eye on him. After that he had to do his army service and that was another blow; because he did not have enough of an education he had to go in as an ordinary soldier and not as an officer. And he being so proud! He fell in with some bad types there, and when he got out he just did not come back very often, except when he was on the run, or needed a refuge, or to get what money he could out of the Contessa."

"Was he actually in prison?"

"Oh, yes," the priest sighed again, "car theft mostly, but once for extortion, an elderly woman, I believe an American."

"So he spoke English."

"Yes, not fluently, but well enough."

"And two years ago, when his father found out about him?"

The priest gave Toby a haunted look. "He was in prison then—he had been picked up as part of a car theft ring."

"And got out about eight months ago?"

"About nine, I think. When he came back here I only saw him the one time and he was much changed. He was proud again and excited, and I know he upset his mother very badly."

"But did he give her or you any indication of his plans?" Toby asked vexedly. "This is the most vital point of all. We have got to find out why he went to America when he did. I mean, where did he get the money to go? Was it from someone over there?"

"He told me nothing—nor his mother, I could swear." Father Antonio looked harried. "But there is one person who *might* be able to tell you. Could you take me into Imola? I will take you to her."

"Right away!" Toby surged to his feet, imparting some of his own sense of urgency to the priest, who hurried with him back to the Bentley, and roared off at a speed that had Father Antonio telling his beads.

"And who is this woman?" Toby asked when they were down the mountain and on the main road to Imola.

"Well, she is someone with whom Lorenzo has been

involved for a great many years. I happen to know about her because just after I came here the Contessa used me as an intermediary to, er, break things up. Lorenzo wanted to marry her, but his mother would not countenance that. The girl was—well, you will see for yourself! Anyway, she made it plain to the girl that if she married Lorenzo she would never be received at the palazzo, nor would he ever see another lira from the Contessa. She also gave the girl quite a sum of money. It worked up to a point: they did not get married, but they have never really broken up, if you follow me. I do hope she hasn't moved," he added anxiously, as they entered the outskirts of Imola. They drove to a mean-looking apartment building in a back street just off the ancient heart of the town, and the priest studied the names on the rusty mailboxes in the hallway with an anxiety replaced by sudden relief. "Ah, she is still there. This way, professore."

He led the way to a grimy doorway which had once been an improbable bright pink. He tapped on it and called softly, "It is Father Antonio, Francesca. Please, I must talk with you!"

The door opened a crack to reveal a pair of dark eyes of a terrible inward blankness, set in a thin, pale face. "What do you want?"

"I must speak with you of Lorenzo."

"That fucking cocksucker!" she said, causing the priest to flinch backward, and she went to close the door. Toby in the best gumshoe tradition hastily jammed a foot in it. "Madam, you'll either talk to us or to the police—take your choice," he boomed.

That did it. She shrugged, flung the door open and turned her back on them, flicking a great mass of dyed blonde, not overly clean hair back over her shoulder. "I might have known!" she said. "Now what has that bastard been up to?"

Toby went in, pushing the unwilling priest ahead of him, and closed the door. They followed her into a cluttered room impregnated with the smell of cheap, stale perfume. "So"—she wheeled to face them—"what do you want of me, busting in here like this! Don't tell me the bum has surfaced at last. If you come from him, I can tell you one thing straight—I want my money back and fast. Him and his promises!" She snorted and tossed her head.

Toby decided shock tactics would be the best way to get anything out of her. "We have every reason to believe that Lorenzo Amalfi is dead—murdered. And if you are at all interested in seeing his murderer caught, or getting any of your money back, it is imperative you tell us everything you know about the circumstances of his trip to America."

She became very still and the blank, hard eyes widened in shock. "Lorenzo—dead?" she whispered.

"I'm afraid so." Toby's voice took on a gentler tone. "I'm sorry to have to break the news like this, but the matter has become an urgent one. If you cared for him at all, please help us."

She sat down slowly, her eyes still dazed. "Oh, Lorenzo!" It came out as a little moan. "What is left for me now?"

"Please!" Toby prompted gently. "He came to you, did he, when he got out of prison? Did he mention hearing from a Rinaldo Dimola?"

"Yes," she said dully, "there was a letter. He was so excited. There had been a man waiting for him when he got out of prison. A private detective, just like something in a movie. He gave him the letter and some money; a long letter, many, many pages—he showed it to me. Oh, it was all about how the man was his real father and how he'd never known because of that fucking bitch at the palazzo, and how he was going to make it up to Lorenzo, and that he was rich—so rich!" A faint glow came into the dark eyes. "Lorenzo was so happy. 'My big chance,' he kept on saying, 'my big chance. Now I'll show them.'"

"Did this letter mention arrangements for going to America?"

"No." She shook her head violently. "His father said he would come out to Rome and meet him and they would talk over his future. He spoke of his second family and how he'd have to prepare them for Lorenzo. But Lorenzo wouldn't wait—couldn't wait. Said he had to go off right away in case the old man thought better of it. 'I've got the right,' he kept on saying, 'I'm his eldest son, he can't send me away—I've got the right.'"

"So his father was not expecting him?"

"No. Lorenzo was going to, like, surprise him. Get all

his travel arrangements made and then just tell him at the last minute. He was pretty sharp, you know."

"But why was he in such a hurry?"

Her face became blankly sullen. "Well, I mean, with all that money the old man had! 'We'll be living on velvet,' Lorenzo kept telling me. And, besides, he'd crossed some people here; he was afraid to stay around in case they got on to him."

Toby scented evasion but did not press. "If the private detective gave him money, why did he need any from you?"

"The money was supposed to keep him going until Big Daddy got here. It was enough for the air fare to America —but there was the passport. He had to buy one under the counter, see, and they don't come cheap!"

"Where did he get it?"

She shrugged. "No idea."

"And what name did he use?"

Again she shrugged. "I don't know—he used several, Salas, Croce—maybe he used Dimola; after all, that *was* his name, he told me. He always stuck to Lorenzo though."

"Well that should help narrow it down," Toby murmured absently. "And do you know whether he went to New York or Boston, and exactly when he left?"

"New York, I think. But I don't know when he went. He left here about mid-September, but he still hadn't got the passport. He was going to get it in Rome—you could get anything there, he said." Her sallow face suddenly became pinched and spiteful. "So what about my money, eh? How'm I going to go about getting that with him dead?"

"If you'll give me your name and address and the amount, I'm sure the Dimola family will take care of that obligation," Toby said stiffly, "although it may take awhile."

"Francesca Volci," she snapped, and added the address and an improbably large sum. "And what am I supposed to do in the meantime? He cleaned me out of everything I had put aside."

Toby checked the impulse to say, "What you evidently have been doing all the time." Although she made his flesh creep he felt sorry for the girl, from whom the flush and attractiveness of youth had long since fled as she had waited around for her erratic lover.

"All this information I've given out," she went on petulantly, "and my time—that doesn't come for nothing, you know. How about it?" With an inward sigh, Toby got out his wallet and took out two large-denomination bills. "This should take care of things for a while."

She took them but suddenly her eyes filled with tears and her face crumpled. "Oh, why did he have to go and die," she sobbed, "just when everything was going to be so nice!"

Father Antonio pressed Toby's arm. "I'll stay with her for a while," he said quietly. "You go on about your business, professore, I'll take care of this and I'll find my own way back. She really did care for him, you know."

Toby—who could not bear to see a woman cry—escaped thankfully, feeling a little guilty about leaving the priest saddled with the problem. Not a bad fellow, he reflected, and I would not have his job if it were the last one on earth.

During the drive back to Colle d'Imola he put his newly acquired information in order and began to think about it. With this new insight the police should rapidly be able to pin down Lorenzo Dimola's entrance into the United States. But then what? In a strange country how would Lorenzo have got from New York to Cape Cod with limited funds? Toby doubted whether he'd have hired a car; it would have needed an international driver's license, which he did not think would be easily available to an ex-convict. But the police could check that too.

He personally favored train or bus—no, there were no trains to the Cape. Bus then—to where? This would be harder to check—no names on bus tickets. And then what would Lorenzo do? Contact his father to say he had arrived and was on his way? But how? The Dimolas' phone was unlisted—something Lorenzo would not know about.

No, wait! He was making a basic mistake. He cursed himself for not asking one important question—the address on the letter—and almost turned the car around but, remembering the sad state of Francesca Volci, decided against it. Penny had said the whole family had been at Masuit only since Rinaldo's illness; chances were Dimola had written from the company's HQ in Boston—so Lorenzo would surely go there to enquire. And would be told precious little he was sure. So here he had Lorenzo wandering around Boston at a dead end and still unsure of his welcome. Toby sighed vexedly, he was getting nowhere, he must start from the other end.

The murderer had met Lorenzo and somehow had lured him to his doom. How? It could not have been by chance. What would Lorenzo have said to Rinaldo in that last-minute letter? Something like, "I will be arriving in New York from Rome, Sat. morning on flight number so-and-so? Hoping to be contacted?" So *if* it was that letter that had given Rinaldo his stroke, then somebody else in the household must have seen it, removed it; *knew*. What would they do? Easy. "Paging Mr. Lorenzo Dimola on flight number so-and so" or perhaps just a message left at the TWA desk. Toby felt a growing inward excitement. At least this was something tangible, a long-distance call from the household which could be checked on. And the murderer would then be calling the shots. "Take the bus (or whatever) to Hyannis and I will meet you there. Father is ill. Will pick you up and take you to him, but we must talk first . . ." Something like that. Then, on the lonely estate, the lulling of suspicion, the sudden blow—and exit Lorenzo.

Drawing up at the inn, he felt satisfied with this and hurried to put in a transatlantic call. Nobody knew where Penny was. Quietly cursing her unflagging energy, Toby got in touch with Detective Eldredge with whom, even at long distance, he had established a rapport. Barney Eldredge was a rare man, a man who knew how to listen, and when Toby had finished said, "Ee-yah, I think you've got a lot there, Professor, we'll get onto it right away. And not to worry about Dr. Spring. I've told her she need not bother herself further. We've got the case in hand now."

When Toby hung up the phone, he sat there frowning at it. Granted that the police dug up the corroboration for his theory, where did it get them? Not very far. It would get Lorenzo to the Masuit estate, it might even give them a shadowy idea as to the identity of the murderer, but how would they ever prove it?

He snorted gently to himself at Detective Eldredge's delusion that Penny was off the case. He knew full well that at this stage it would be like taking a catnip mouse away from an intoxicated cat. She'd be right there—probably one step ahead of them, but what could she do about proving it either?"

Suddenly he grew rigid, sat up, took his pipe out of his mouth and glared wildly at the phone. "My God!" he said, "I know *exactly* what she'll try and do. I've got to get over there before it's too late . . ."

CHAPTER 20

"You realize I could get permanently canned for what you're asking me to do." Carson Grange made it a statement rather than a question.

"If I could think of any other way, or if you weren't so heavily involved already, I wouldn't even ask, but can *you* see any other solution?" Penny countered.

Carson was silent, but whether from reflection or exhaustion it was hard to tell; it seemed they had been arguing for hours. Ann had returned in the middle of the argument, and with monumental tact had removed herself and the children to McDonald's, leaving the arena clear for the two protagonists. "It may not even work and we would have stuck both our necks out for nothing," he said finally.

"Agreed. The murderer is wary now with all the police finally looking in this direction but must be feeling increasingly desperate too. Wanda's killing was a panic murder if ever I saw one. Luckily none of them know as yet how much we have turned up at the Italian end or how rapidly the net is closing. But the direct *proof* may never be forthcoming and they may get away scot-free if we can't jolt them into showing their hand. As I've already said, Rinaldo won't tell, Zeb can't, and, even if he could, probably wouldn't, as you well know. Who else is there to point the finger? I'm convinced Eagle Smith is telling the truth when he says he saw no one that day. With Wanda gone and the other business out in the open now, there is no reason he would lie about that, since it would let him definitely off the hook too. So what's left? It's useless to bring the police officially in on this; they'd never stand for it because, I suppose, it *is* a form of entrapment."

"A highly dangerous form of entrapment," Carson put in drily.

"Perhaps. And that's precisely why, if I am to be bait for the tiger, I'd like someone backing me up who has and can use a gun. I know it is asking you to take a big risk, but you know as well as I do that, unless we solve this case, there's going to be a cloud of suspicion surrounding you from now on, which can only harm you."

He nodded gloomily. "Yes, I can see that all right. My ex-wife, who doesn't miss much, has already started to make noises about Bobby's custody again. So, O.K., suppose I do go along, what kind of a setup have you got in mind?"

Penny frowned. "There again I've got the general outline but not the details. It would have to be at night and at the Grange house. At night, because if you're going to be backup you'd never be able to get close enough to the house in the day to be of any help—there's just not enough near cover."

"Why couldn't I just hide inside?"

"Too risky. If I were the murderer, the first thing I'd do would be to check the rest of the house before going after me in the museum room—and there's nowhere *in* the room you could hide."

"Why has it to be there anyway?"

Penny ran her hands through her short, mouse-colored hair until it stood up in spikes. "Because, although it's a bit thin, it's the only story I can think up that the murderer might go for. Written evidence hidden there that I'll be searching for. I thought first of a message from Wanda, because no one did search the room again after her murder, but the murderer might know Wanda did not have much to tell, so I'll use Zeb; some nonsense about coming out of his coma and asking for me and then muttering about evidence hidden in one of the Indian pots."

Carson looked skeptical. "Surely no one would go for that! I mean, it's so corny."

Penny shrugged helplessly. "I know, but I've told you who I suspect and why, and, if they're as desperate as I think, they simply can't afford to take a chance on it. We can't just rush off and do this, the timing will have to be exactly right to look natural. I'll have to show up at the mansion all excited and self-important, blurt out the 'big news,' and take off for the house, hoping the murderer will rise to the bait."

"And your idea is for me to lurk about outside until

somebody does follow you into the house, then wait a minute or two and follow—is that right?"

"Exactly."

"You'll be taking one hell of a risk—you know that?"

"I know, but I'm banking on a certain element of surprise *and* the murderer's vanity to keep things inactive until you get there." She grinned weakly at him. "Are you on?"

There was no answering smile on his face but, "I'm on," he agreed. "When?"

"Can you take a couple of days off? Either tomorrow or the day after. The day after that is the inquest on Wanda, which I could use as an excuse to go to the mansion with my 'big news.' "

"Yes, I can get leave, but what'll I do with myself?" he grumbled.

This time her grin was impish. "Why don't you hang around here? You seem to like the company."

"I'm not going to have Ann dragged into this," he glowered at her, "she's had enough trouble."

"No, indeed!" Penny agreed with fervor, "it would be better if she didn't know a thing about it." Seeing the evident relief on his face, she did not add what she was thinking: that Ann's ignorance would not be so much for her safety as for their own.

When she did make her assault on the Dimola family citadel she was fully expecting to find them a little at odds with one another. They were far from dim-witted, and the events of the last few days must have shown them that the finger of suspicion was now turned to someone in their own household. She expected to find them fearful and suspicious of one another—but she was quite unprepared to walk into a flaming family row, which almost took the wind out of her sails and spoiled her carefully prepared act. The irony lay in that the row had nothing to do with the case at all.

She had gone into her act the moment the fortresslike door had opened, brushing past the startled manservant and demanding excitedly to see Alexander "with important news." Hearing loud voices from the direction of the drawing room she had barged on, leaving the man spluttering feebly in the rear, and burst in on a dramatic scene. Maria, her color flaring, her eyes flashing, was standing embattled in front of the fireplace, an unknown and solemn young man by her side, who in turn was flanked by a tense-faced Annette. Ranged like an opposing force opposite to them were Alexander, Steven and Inga, all looking furious. They were all talking at once, but stopped in mid-sentence to wheel in unison on her intrusion. Penny, inwardly more than a little nonplussed, felt it was too late to withdraw, so plunged on with the act. "Mr. Dimola, I'm sorry to barge in on you like this, but I have most important news . . ." she began, but was not allowed to finish.

"Dr. Spring," Maria burst out, "I appeal to you as one who has seen my father! Would you not say that he would rather risk death than continue as he is?"

"I call a thirty-five per cent chance of success more than a *risk*," Steven snarled with cold anger. "The whole idea is insane."

"You want to kill him, you want him dead," shrilled Inga at her sister-in-law.

Maria whirled on her, "It is *you* who must want him dead," she shouted. "Why did we ever listen to you and those stupid doctors! If it had been done immediately, as Dr. Lavin here has said, the chances for success would have been much greater, but now, even after all this time, I say it is still what Poppa wishes—you have seen that he *does* wish it. To have a chance to move again, to speak again, however slim—do you not think he wants that rather than the living hell he has now! He would rather die than go on like this! If you have any feelings for him at all, you must see that!"

The young man beside Maria suddenly held up both hands in an appeal for silence. "Please!" he commanded in a rather high tenor voice. "This is getting us nowhere. Let me restate the case and my position in it, particularly now that there is another doctor who can confirm my statements." Penny opened her mouth to correct him, then quietly shut it again as he went on. "There are undispersed clots from the cerebral hemorrhage resting on your father's brain cortex. After this length of time the only way to remove them is by surgery. The risk is high, as I have indicated, but without it the likelihood of recovery to a state much beyond what he is in now is remote. From my two visits to the patient, I am satisfied that he is aware of what surgery entails and does wish it. However, I have no intention of proceeding without consulting another specialist in the field, who must also convince himself of Mr. Dimola's wishes, and even then we would not proceed without the full *written* consent of Mrs. Rinaldo Dimola, which, preferably but not *necessarily* I may point out, would have the approval of the rest of the family."

"Oh, you'll get *hers* all right, for wouldn't she be the merry widow, wouldn't she just!" hissed Inga with surprising venom.

Annette's pale face went a shade paler, as Steven suddenly roared, "Be quiet, Inga! You've said enough." The icy blue eyes turned on him with cold anger, but the terrible cold flame died, and Inga subsided, muttering to herself. Annette spoke for the first time, her voice low and troubled. "I have already said, Dr. Lavin, since it is evidently what my husband desires, that I would give the necessary consent, but I would want additional opinions."

The doctor gave an abrupt nod. "Well then, I will leave now. When you have decided, call my office and I will send you a list of surgeons from which you can choose a further consultant. They will be the best in the field. Good night to you all." He gave a stiff bow and escaped from the room with evident relief.

There was a momentary silence after he left as the combatants glared at one another, and Penny could feel the wave of hostility, the throbbing of raw nerves, that filled the room with almost unbearable emotion. Then Alexander came to with a start and turned to her. "I'm sorry, but you have caught us at rather a bad moment, Dr. Spring. Did you say something about important news?"

Feeling a terrible sense of anticlimax, Penny struggled to put verve back into her act. "Yes, well, I thought I should tell you about this latest important development— Zeb emerged briefly from his coma and called for me. Unfortunately by the time they found me and I got to the hospital, he was slipping back into it again. But I did make sense of some of his mutterings"—she tried to sound breathlessly excited—"apparently he wrote down what happened this fall after I had been here. It has to do with the body in the bog. He hid what he wrote, apparently in the museum room; he didn't say where before he became unconscious again. Since we've already been through all the papers there, he must have hidden it in one of the Indian pots. I'm going over to the house now to search for it. It is even possible your wife knew something of it, Mr. Dimola, since she made the museum room our ill-fated rendezvous. In any case, when I find it, it will be invaluable evidence which will probably come out at the inquest. I just thought you ought to know."

They were all staring at her as if the news had not quite penetrated their other preoccupation and they were patiently waiting for her to finish and be gone. Penny mentally cursed an unkind fate, as Alexander stared at her with slightly blank, troubled eyes. "Er, you want some one of us to assist you?"

"Oh, no," she said hastily, "no need at all. I'm sorry to have disturbed such a private family discussion. I'll be off."

"There is no need to rush off on that account," Annette put in in a voice devoid of all emotion. "I feel that we should postpone any further discussion until we have all cooled down and slept on the matter. I, for one, am going to do just that. I'll see you to the door." She swept through the room, not looking at any of the others, and taking Penny's elbow steered her firmly out. As she opened the front door she looked at Penny with veiled eyes. "I will do it for him, not for me," she said. "I think he wishes to be dead, and maybe it is better so."

Outside it had begun to snow; great white flakes that slapped and stung but which did not settle on the wet black earth. Penny hurried to where the car was parked away from the house and dived into its welcome warmth. "How did it go?" Carson's voice came out of the darkness. He had a dark seaman's jacket on over his uniform, which rendered him almost invisible.

"I don't know." She shivered. "Not too well I'm afraid. And damn this snow! That won't help at all, the murderer might not want to risk it."

"It won't settle, not while it's this wet," Carson said with certainty, "but do you want to call it off?"

"No, it's too late now. We may as well go on with it. If nothing happens we'll have to try something else."

They drove in silence to the Grange house. "I'll wait by the path that had the bicycle tracks," Carson volunteered.

"I think it's the most likely route, and I can keep an eye on the rest of the clearing from the big oak there. How long shall we give it?"

"I think if anything is going to happen, it will happen fairly quickly." Penny was subdued. "The murderer isn't going to risk me finding something and taking off with it. Let's say an hour at the outside."

"Going to be a mighty cold hour," Carson sighed, and slipped into the night.

She let herself into the house, with little chills running up her spine that had nothing to do with the raw night outside. When the orange cat, who had slipped inside with her but unseen, rubbed itself against her legs, she almost screamed, but quieted her throbbing heart and gave him some milk in the kitchen, where she made certain the back door was locked and bolted so that the only possible ingress to the house would be the front. She took a quick glance through all the rooms, then went up to the museum room, switched on the desk light and prepared to set the stage. She took a few pots from the cabinets and ranged them on the desk, then scattered some sheets of notes from the files among the pots. This done, she sat down and steeled herself to wait. The cat jumped into her lap and, eyes closed in bliss, began kneading it, purring loudly.

The minutes stretched out and with them her nerves. Nothing happened. She wondered now how wise she had been in spinning Detective Eldredge her fairy tale of going off to Boston. She had contacted him and heard about Toby's findings concerning Lorenzo, but to quiet any suspicions he might still harbor about her own activities had told him she was off to Boston, destination unspecified. Then she thought she heard a muffled thud from somewhere below and started slightly, disturbing the now-sleeping cat, who jumped down swishing his tail. She strained her ears, but there was nothing save the light patter of the snow against the windows and the wintry creakings of the old house. She kept her eyes glued on the closed door, her mouth dry with apprehension. I wish I'd brought something to munch on, she was thinking, when the doorknob began to turn slowly.

The door swung open, revealing a large shadow outlined

against the wall, and then someone stood on the threshold shining a flashlight into her eyes. Even in her rising fear, Penny felt a small thrill of triumph as she knew she had been right. "Come on in," she said, in a voice that sounded strange to her, "I was expecting you . . ."

CHAPTER 21

At first the fates had been kind to Toby; he had packed and got out of Colle d'Imola in record time. He had driven to Bologna, dumped the Bentley on a startled archaeological colleague with the injunction to guard it until his return, and had found a quick flight to Rome. There came the first hitch: no plane until the following afternoon, when he would have the choice of several; he chose the Rome-Chicago flight, which stopped in Boston.

During his enforced wait he fumed and fretted as to what he should do. He tried several times to reach Penny at the Dimola number with no success; the household at that end seemed upset and confused, which did nothing to lift his spirits. Despairing of reaching her direct, he thought about an appeal to the state police, but then decided against that too. Knowing her as well as he did, he thought that whatever Penny was up to was probably not legal at all, and if he put the state police on to her it would mean (a) she would never forgive him for ruining her plans, and (b) she might get in serious legal trouble herself.

To quiet his own jumping nerves and conscience, however, he did call Detective Eldredge again to enquire cautiously how things were going. They were going splendidly, he was informed. Lorenzo Dimola had already been traced to New York, there *had* been a long-distance call from the Dimola house to the TWA desk with a message, but they still had no definite information on what the message contained or the identity of the caller. "But early days yet, and so far the progress is excellent," Barnabas Eldredge enthused. "We are greatly indebted to you, Professor Glendower, for the leads."

"Er, have you any idea where I might get in touch with Dr. Spring?" Toby ventured. "I don't seem to be able to reach her at the Dimola estate."

"None, I'm afraid. Did say something though about

going into Boston." Eldredge was unrelentingly cheerful. "Be back in time for the inquest tomorrow, for sure, Barnstable Courthouse, 11 o'clock. Could try her there."

"Well, if she does happen to contact you," Toby said with forlorn hope, "would you give her a message from me? Tell her I'm on my way and to do *nothing* about what she has in mind until I see her."

"You're coming over here!" There was shocked surprise in the detective's voice.

"Er, yes, just on personal business; Dr. Spring will understand," Toby said a little desperately.

"Oh, yes, well I'll surely do that. Come and see us when you get here, be glad to fill you in," Eldredge assured, and rang off.

Toby almost groaned as he put down the phone; whatever Penny was up to she was doing it on her own without any official knowledge or blessing. He only hoped that her natural curiosity would drive her to call the police in time for his message to do some good.

It seemed the fates were still smiling when he took off from Rome on time a couple of hours later, but they turned perverse just as the flight reached Boston. "There will be a delay in landing," the pilot's bland voice announced over the intercom, "due to a pileup of incoming traffic over Logan. A snowstorm is moving in from the west. We will fly a holding pattern until cleared for landing."

This went on for an hour, and the early darkness had fallen by the time the plane rolled to a stop before the lighted terminal. Toby was seized with an increasing sense of urgency; it would take ages to get a car and find his way to the benighted fastnesses of the Cape—and time was of the essence. He had spent the agonized waiting time above the roiling snow clouds rereading Penny's letters. John Everett, Penny's publisher—he would contact him and get him to drive him down to the Cape. Once there, he had a sketch map Penny had sent him of the Dimola estate, and, if she was to be found, he would find her.

Once through customs and immigration he rushed to the nearest phone and called John Everett at his office, praying it would not be closed. This time luck was with him: John Everett was working late. "You don't know me, Mr. Everett," he boomed into the phone, "but I'm Toby Glendower, Penny Spring's colleague, just in from Rome. You haven't seen her here in Boston by any chance?" On being assured not, he trumpeted on, "I have reason to believe she may be in some danger, and since I know you are a good friend of hers, I wonder if you could pick me up at the airport here and take me down to the Cape. I feel it is very urgent and you know the way and I don't."

"What danger do you think she is in?" Everett sounded concerned but unsurprised.

"I think she is probably laying a trap for the murderer— by herself."

"Good Lord!" Now there was genuine alarm in Everett's voice. "Hang on, I'll be right there. Meet me outside the TWA entrance—a bright green Triumph Spitfire. Be about twenty minutes, if I'm lucky."

As Toby went outside the first great white snowflakes began to fall from the scudding, leaden clouds above. John Everett was as good as his word, and the short, roly-poly man and the long, lanky one, after the briefest of greetings, somehow poured themselves into the tiny car and sped off. Toby looked anxiously at the falling snow. "Will this slow us down much?"

John Everett cast an expert eye at the heavens. "Coming in from the west. We may even keep ahead of it. Probably hasn't even started on the Cape yet. Won't settle anyway, too wet. What is this all about?"

Tersely Toby outlined the situation and his conclusions. "Penny has probably already seen that, with the known facts, the police will be able to get so far but no further. Knowing her, I think she'll try to lure the murderer out of cover by using herself as bait in some way. I only hope to God she got my message and won't try anything until we get there."

"You're right"—Everett's voice was full of gloomy foreboding—"she would never just fade quietly off the scene as the state detective thinks. Well, let's hope she did get the message or that we're in time." And floored the accelerator.

They reached Masuit in a little over an hour, and as they drove through the scatter of lights in the hamlet, John

Everett said, "Where do we make for now, the Dimola mansion?"

"No, let's try Ann Langley's cottage first," Toby said, peering at the sketch map by the dim light of the dashboard. "It's where she was staying, and even if she isn't in, Ann might know where she is and what's she's up to. I only hope this sketch map is accurate!"

At a slower pace, they plunged into the dark fastnesses of the estate, until a welcome gleam of light showed to their left among the close-ranked trees. With audible sighs of relief they scrunched to a stop next to a parked station wagon and a battered Volkswagen and piled stiffly out of the car.

Their arrival had been heard and a light went on over the door of the cottage, a curtain pulled back in a window. Then the door was flung open and the frightened face of Ann Langley appeared. "Dr. Glendower!" she cried. "What on earth are you doing here?"

He loped up to her. "Ann, where's Dr. Spring? I've got to find her at once."

She fell back and held the door open as he and John Everett entered. Toby introduced Everett, then anxiously, "Is she here?"

"Why no—she's with Carson Grange. I've no idea where they are. Carson came around earlier and asked if I'd babysit Bobby for him." She waved a vague hand in the direction of a pretty little girl and a plain little boy who were completely absorbed in a complicated mass of building blocks on the floor.

Toby and John looked at one another with relief. "At least she has got a man with her," Toby said. "That's something."

"A policeman," a voice corrected from the floor. "My dad's a policeman. He's got a gun and everything."

John Everett heaved a sigh of relief. "Even better! So at least she's safe for the moment. Now we just have to wait for them to get back."

Toby continued to gaze in concern at Ann. "They gave you no idea of where they were going or what they were doing?"

She shook her head. "No. They just took off, oh, about an hour to an hour and a half ago."

"*I* know," continued the persistent voice from the floor.

"You do, Bobby?" Ann quavered in surprise.

"Yes, they were going to Uncle Zeb's house."

"Why were they going there, dear?"

The small boy gave an exaggerated imitation of an adult shrug. "I dunno. Catch a crook maybe? Dad was in his uniform—got his gun too."

"Are you sure?" There was fear in her voice as the two men glanced at one another uneasily.

"That's where they *said,*" Bobby Grange insisted in a voice permeated with the consciousness of adult vagaries in these matters.

"I think we ought to get over there," Toby said abruptly. "Could you show us the way, Ann? It would save time."

She dithered. "I can't leave the children alone."

"Well bring them then." Toby was testy. "You can take them in your car, we'll follow you, and as soon as we get to the house you can bring them home again."

"Oh, all right," she said reluctantly. There was a small delay as the protesting children were bundled into winter coats and Ann put on her own, then the little safari squelched off into the night.

"At least she's got someone with her," John Everett repeated hopefully.

Toby grunted. "The last time she went careering off with someone like that she damn nearly got herself killed—*he* was the murderer."

"Oh!" Everett lapsed into startled silence until the car's lights swept the cleared area in which the Grange house stood, then he let out a yelp. "There's somebody lying on the front porch—see!"

Before the car had completely rolled to a stop they were both out of it and running toward the huddled mound before the front door. Toby knelt and turned the still figure over. "It's the policeman," he muttered. "Knocked out by the look of it—see the ugly cut on his forehead."

Footsteps pattered behind them and Ann flew up onto the porch and gave a little scream. "Oh, no! Not Carson! Is he dead?"

Toby shook his head as he undid the dark jacket with fumbling frantic fingers. "Oh my God, his gun's gone!" he moaned, and leaping to his feet let out a stentorian bellow, "Penny!"

Just as he shouted there came the report of a gun from somewhere upstairs in the darkened house—three times it shattered the silence, as they stood rooted to the spot with shock. "Penny!" Toby yelled again, and bounding in through the door, started to stumble up the dark stairs.

John Everett, with magnificent presence of mind, found the switch which flooded the stairs and porch with light, yelled "Stay here!" to the immobile Ann, and followed Toby up the stairs.

As they burst into the only room from which a faint light showed, they saw the figure of a man with a gun in his hand bending over the form of a woman on the floor; a large flashlight, lying on the floor beside her, illumined the head—or what was left of it—bringing forth the golden glint of blonde hair. They stood transfixed as he rose slowly, the gun dropping from his nerveless fingers onto the bare polished floor with a metallic finality. A blank face turned toward them. "I had to do it," the quiet, expressionless voice said, "I had to kill her—it was a matter of family honor, you see."

It's not Penny, it's not Penny, was all Toby's dazed mind could register. "Who is she? Whom did you kill?" he muttered stupidly.

"My wife, I killed my wife," said Steven Dimola, and began to weep.

Toby looked around at the shattered glass cases, at the bits of shattered pottery and stone tools lying all over the floor—evidence of a fight, one hell of a fight. "Penny," he said woodenly, "where is she?"

There was a slight scrabbling noise from behind the big desk and a small head wobbled cautiously into view, backlit by an overturned lamp on the floor. Apart from a small cut on her forehead and an extreme state of dishevellment, Penny appeared to be more or less intact. "Here I am," she croaked groggily. "Shooting all over? Fancy seeing you here, Toby. Nice timing. Oh, hello, John, you here too for the finale? Just like old home week." She wobbled over to a chair and sat down in it very abruptly. "Well! That was quite a fight—and a bit more than I bargained for."

"One of these days," Toby snarled, severe in his relief,

"you're going to get yourself killed for certain, and you'll ruddy well deserve it too!"

John Everett, who had picked up the gun and had it trained rather nervously on the still, silently sobbing figure of Steven Dimola, started suddenly and swung toward the door as footsteps clattered up the stairs. Ann Langley appeared on the threshold, her face blanching in terror as she took in the shambles. "No, no, no!" she screamed, "not you, Steven—it isn't, it *couldn't* be you!" and rushed at him.

"Don't!" Penny commanded sharply. "Don't, Ann! Steven had to do it. He saved my life. Inga would have killed me just as she had killed twice before; Inga was the murderer, Ann, not Steven."

CHAPTER 22

Naturally there had been hell to pay. The state police had arrived first, headed by Detective Eldredge, who looked as if he would willingly have committed murder himself given the slightest encouragement. The most likely candidate would have been Carson, but since the latter was still unconscious Eldredge was reduced to muttering darkly under his breath as he watched the rescue squad cart Carson off to join his uncle in the hospital, the police doctor having diagnosed a concussion.

The Barnstable police arrived with the rescue squad, adding to the general air of confusion, and Detective Thompson, faced with yet another body in his jurisdiction, was equalling Eldredge in the murderous looks and feelings department.

Steven Dimola had been taken into custody, but even then it was not plain sailing for the beleaguered police. In view of Penny's adamant testimony that he had shot his wife to save her own life, they couldn't charge him with murder. They dithered on about manslaughter, until John Everett primly pointed out that they would run into serious difficulties there, since, in his opinion, to kill a felon in order to prevent a murder could hardly be construed as manslaughter. Bemused with all these ardent amateur criminologists, the police had finally, and rather lamely, charged Steven with "the theft of a deadly weapon and its unlawful firing on private premises," and hoped to improve on the situation later.

Within the hour, Alexander had come charging to his brother's rescue like some medieval knight, flanked by a battery of lawyers, and Steven was once again a free, if shattered, man.

Both police forces would willingly have incarcerated Penny and thrown away the key, but could think of no valid reason to arrest her and were considerably hampered by the apparent fact that she had, at one fell swoop, solved all their most thorny cases for them. Of course they had given her a hard time, but she was so bucked up by her own success that she gave as good as she got, supplied them with all of the statements and explanations she thought was good for them to know, and emerged still tousled but triumphant from the ordeal.

Toby and John Everett stood helplessly by during the badgering, since they had to be studiedly vague about their own fortuitous arrival on the scene lest they get Penny into even deeper hot water than she was already in. But, finally, it was over. The police retreated, bearing with them the body of the murderer; the dazed Ann took her sleeping little charges back to the cottage; and Penny, Toby and John wearily sought sanctuary in a Hyannis motel. "I'll tell you the whole story tomorrow," the groggy Penny had promised, and falling into bed had slept for twelve straight hours.

They had had to feed her first, but after she had munched her way through an enormous lunch she sat back with a happy sigh. "Ahh! I feel a whole lot better. So, explanation time is here, I guess. By the way, I can't thank you two enough for arriving when you did, you most probably saved another life."

John Everett looked at her open-mouthed. "You mean Steven Dimola *was* involved after all?"

She shook her head. "No, but if you hadn't come charging in when you did I think he may well have turned the gun on himself. Basically he was very fond of her, you know, which is probably why he allowed himself to be blinded to what she was really up to for so long. I'm so glad he wasn't involved. I thought for a while they were both in it, but she put my mind at rest on that last night."

"What made you so certain it was she?"

Penny looked at Toby with a bright eye. "I wasn't until you supplied me with three crowning facts: Lorenzo's legitimacy, his imprisonment and his trip over here—then a whole lot of details fell into place. For one thing Steven and Inga would have had the most to lose by the arrival of the new heir. Steven was the apple of his father's eye *only* because he was the seeming elder, for in other respects they had nothing in common: the doer and the nondoer, the dynamic and the passive. Inga was shrewd enough to realize this. She was also greedy, possessive, not overly bright and insecure—the theft of the photo and the ransacking of Ann's cottage show that. With Lorenzo taking the crown as eldest son Steven would have been reduced to just another rich dilettante——"

"I would have thought Alexander would have been just as likely a suspect," Toby interposed. *"He,* by all accounts, is a man of action and more likely to have taken drastic steps against a threat to the family or his position than Steven."

"Yes, but I never thought about Alexander too seriously," Penny continued brightly. "After all, there's the name —I never think anyone called Alexander could do anything very wrong."

Toby cast his eyes to heaven in silent entreaty against her magnificent illogic and retreated behind his pipe again.

"And besides, he is so valuable to his father, nothing really could threaten his position," she went on. "To all intents and purposes he *is* Dimola Enterprises, so his motive was less. Also I was certain he did not kill his wife and, of course, he didn't fit the bill in other respects too. Let me go on." She brushed aside an attempted question.

"They had the motive. As to the means: well, I knew they had all been to Imola in Rinaldo's wake. They may have surmised about Christiana Amalfi, they may have even guessed at a child, in view of Rinaldo's changed behavior, but *none* of them could have known for sure about Lorenzo's legitimacy *unless* they had seen that letter announcing his unexpected arrival, the letter that precipitated Rinaldo's stroke. No letter was ever found, but who discovered Rinaldo that day slumped over his desk in the study? *Inga!*

"She probably had been watching Rinaldo closely ever since he had 'cheered up,' as Annette Dimola told me, shortly before. After all, Rinaldo thought he had things in hand, was about to fly out to Rome to make amends to this unknown son of his first love, who so far had had such a disastrous and shameful life. Probably he was planning to settle a large sum on him and start him off on a new life in another country, but *not here.*

"Then comes catastrophe! Lorenzo jumps the gun and is on his way to claim his rightful place in a family unaware of his existence. The shock is too much for Rinaldo, who has a stroke. Inga finds the letter. Inga realizes in a flash what it means to her own position. In the confusion after Rinaldo's stroke she realizes that if she can get to Lorenzo first and fast to silence him no one need ever know. She phones New York and sets up a rendezvous. 'Your father is ill, I'm your sister-in-law, and I'll meet you at Hyannis bus terminal and take you right to him' or some such likely story. Lorenzo might have been wary of his half brothers, but the news must have been an awful shock to him too, remember, and he'd no reason to suspect her of any ulterior motives—so he comes.

"She meets him and sees the striking resemblance to Rinaldo. Now she has a further problem; not only must she kill him but she must be sure the body is not found. She drives him to the estate and, with almost a touch of genius, takes him to the one place where he can be quickly hidden —the Indian site where there are ready-made graves dug to order, much safer than, say, the marsh or the bog where the body might be found and identified.

"I imagine another factor entered in here. I think she was well aware of Wanda's drug taking and drug pick up activities. Since we found a Speed capsule in the grave this may well have been one of Wanda's pick-up points Inga knew about. So, after braining Lorenzo with a shovel, she hides the body in *that* grave, banking on the fact that Wanda and Eagle Smith, seeing the grave had been newly disturbed, would just think it was the other one's doing.

"Up to that point everything had gone her way, then it began to go sour. She had not banked on Zeb's eagle eye nor on his obsessive concern about those Indian graves. Undoubtedly she left some kind of private markings on the grave to satisfy herself that no one had been messing in it —leastways, that's what *I* would have done. So. She learns to her horror that Zeb has found the body, but still all is not lost. She moves the body, making sure this time that no one will identify it by mutilating the face. To make doubly sure the troubled Zeb does not have a chance to get together with Rinaldo she persuades the family to bring Rinaldo home and to dismiss the professional nurses. In that she did succeed and I think, if it had not been for the persistent Maria, Rinaldo may never have improved at all under her 'care.'

"But, in spite of her, he did improve a little. The words he tried to say made no sense to Maria, but they did to Inga, who of course knew Lorenzo's name; so at that juncture she probably quieted her father-in-law by saying that *Steven* had taken care of the matter and he was not to worry.

"Then comes her second catastrophe—the second finding of the body. Zeb, poor soul, is finally roused to action, and my ill-advised attempts to get in touch with him alert her for the first time to the fact that he may be about to tell someone else what he has found. From this point she becomes panicky. She tries to 'arrange' the accident, but is scared off by Eagle Smith before she succeeds. Zeb is out of action, but I arrive and start sniffing around to little purpose. She is scared now, but still safe—perhaps even more so after the inquest when Maria reveals to her father the facts of the inquest and which shows Rinaldo that the body in the bog must be Lorenzo's. Then Inga's assurance to him that 'Steven had taken care of the matter' takes on a new and terrible meaning, which I'm sure she reinforced —hence his absolute refusal to try to communicate with me about it.

"Eagle Smith's arrest for the attack on Zeb was a mixed blessing to her. While it diverted the police to the wrong track, it didn't get me off her back and, worse, it finally aroused the flaky Wanda into action. Again, I feel panic made Inga commit an unnecessary murder. Remember she couldn't be sure who was in the barn that day she attacked Zeb; Eagle Smith, Wanda or both. She couldn't be *sure* whether she'd been seen or not. So when Wanda set up that appointment with me I think she followed her on the bicycle to find out what she was up to; Wanda probably acted surprised and guilty when she turned up, so she killed her out of hand. Her 'alibi' was that she was sitting with Rinaldo—but the only person to have gainsaid that would have been Rinaldo, who in the circumstances wouldn't, and there are literally dozens of ways she could slip out of the house unseen through all those glass doors. So, no problem there.

"But this centered the police's attention really for the

first time on the estate, and she must have been getting pretty desperate and not thinking clearly—otherwise I would never have gotten away with my little charade."

"Why on earth did you take such a *risk?*" John Everett interrupted. "I mean, there must have been a safer way of smoking her out."

Penny grinned sideways at Toby, who was puffing on his pipe and looking resigned. "Well none that occurred to me, and I had to act quickly. You, see, as soon as I got all the vital bits of information together, I realized the same thing that brought Toby here hurtling across the Atlantic; after they had traced Lorenzo to the estate, and even when the motive became apparent, *proving* what had happened to him would have been well-nigh impossible. It was all so long ago that time was on her side—who would remember a woman at a bus terminal or identify a voice over a telephone after six months? So I had to act to force her to show her hand *before* she knew all that we knew. Hence all the rigmarole I went through about a hidden statement of Zeb's. I don't think it would have fooled anyone in their right mind, but by that time she was just about round the bend with worry."

"But the risk of it!" Everett continued to fuss.

"I thought I'd taken care of that by bringing Carson along. The idea was to let her come in, give her a little time to make her move on me, and then for Carson to appear and save the day. Neither of us anticipated that she was so hyper by that time, that she'd lurk inside the door to see no one had followed her, and, when she did see him, would conk him on the head with the big flashlight before coming up to finish me off at her leisure."

Toby took the pipe out of his mouth and broke his silence. "What exactly did happen in that room. I mean, I know what you told the police but, damn it, she was twice your size and very strong, how did you manage to keep out of her way so long?"

"I got lucky," Penny grinned at him again. "When she came storming in, the first thing she said was, 'So you set a trap you - - - bitch, but it won't do you any good.' So I knew at once the jig was up; that she'd seen Carson and dealt with him somehow and I was on my own. She came toward me. I swept the desk lamp on the floor, trying to get out of the light, and then she tripped over the damned cat, who was scooting for the door. She went down. Her flashlight, which must have been damaged when she conked Carson, went out, and it gave me the time to get from behind the desk. I was going to make a run for the door, but she got between me and it and and her flashlight went on again. Then we had a right royal game of dodge-'ems; me throwing pots, tools, anything I could lay hands on, and scurrying around like a demented cat to keep out of her way——"

"Then how come, with all this going on, she confessed?" Toby interrupted.

"That's just it, she never did confess to me, she confessed to *Steven,* who literally did arrive in the nick of time. I had run out of things to throw and she had got me backed up in a corner, her hands around my neck, when he turned up in the doorway with Carson's gun. He just stood and yelled at her, 'Stop it. What in God's name do you think you're doing!' and she kept right on throttling me and yelled back, 'She knows too much, I've got to do it. She knows about the others.' It struck him all of a heap, but I kicked her in the shins and managed to break loose again and gasp out, 'She means she murdered Wanda and your half brother and now will kill me too.' She lunged for me again and then he brought the gun up and shouted, 'If you don't stop, I'll shoot.'

"That seemed to drive her berserk. She pushed me down and rushed at him, screaming, 'Don't you see, you fool, I did it for you! I did it all for you. And if you don't help me now, I'll say you were in it with me all along. It's what I've told your father, and it's what they'll believe!' " Penny stopped abruptly and then went on in a quiet voice, "And then he shot her. I've never seen such a terrible look on anyone's face as I saw on his when he pulled that trigger. I know what 'to look like death' means now." She shivered. "Three times he shot her—the last time in the head as she lay at his feet. Then you came in—and, well, you know the rest.

They all three sat quiet for a moment until John Everett cleared his throat nervously. "So what do you think will happen now?"

"Not much, I hope," Penny said with fervor. "I'm banking on Alexander to bring the heavy Dimola guns to bear and to quiet things down as much as possible. They may get Steven for manslaughter—but I doubt it. The one I'm worried about is Carson; I've put him in a terrible position. I meant to have him covered with glory after capturing the murderer, instead I've landed him in hospital with concussion and in danger of being booted out of his job. Still—" she brightened—"at least I've cleared him of all the suspicion he was under, and he's young enough to get another kind of job if Alexander can't or won't help him. He ought to do something with children, he is terribly good with them."

"You're incorrigible, absolutely incorrigible," Toby sighed. "One thing I'm certain of—as soon as humanly possible I'm going to drag you out of here before you get into any more trouble."

"Oh, where are you proposing to drag me?" Penny was interested.

"To Italy—where you *should* have been all along," he said severely. "There's still ten days of vacation left, thanks to the enlightened policies of the University of Oxford. I have to pick up the car—not to mention a couple of cases of wine from my good friend Enrico. Besides, I'd like you to see Colle d'Imola where all this started."

"Yes." Penny was thoughtful again. "From the start of this case the accent has been on youth; Rinaldo's youth reached out to him and touched his life with its tragedy; my youth, in the shape of Zeb, reached out to me and caused me to be the unwitting Nemesis for all the young people involved in the case. It has brought tragedy to them too—but I only hope some good will come of it. They must all hate me, so I don't suppose I'll ever know the outcome." In that she was wrong.

CHAPTER 23

It took them four days of smooth, fast talking and some good solid help from John Everett to get themselves disentangled from officialdom, then, as threatened, Toby firmly took Penny off to Italy over her agonized protests that she hadn't even seen Alex and couldn't they stay another day or two.

In Bologna they picked up the Bentley and drove up to Colle d'Imola to collect Toby's promised wine. They arrived to find the village in a mild state of ferment over the Contessa's recent demise. Though they had loathed her in life the locals were prepared to mourn her now, for her going had further stripped the village of status and acclaim; the title had died with her, and maternal cousins, who had inherited the ruins of the palazzo, had come, taken one look at it and gone again, declaring that the state was welcome to it so far as they were concerned. Now the villagers had their heads together making rather improbable plans for restoring it themselves and opening it as a tourist hotel.

Toby led Penny to the quiet cemetery where a newly dug mound of earth scattered with a few wilting flowers stood beside the memorial to Christiana Amalfi. They looked at it in silence for a minute or two, then Penny asked, "No family vault?"

"Destroyed in the war."

"Hmm, what a curious woman she must have been. You can't conceive of a hate that great, somehow. What did you make of her?"

Toby grunted. "Since this case has also had overtones of Dante throughout, I came across a description in Benvenuto D'Imola's book on him that fitted her very well. 'A woman called Ciangbella,' he quoted, 'an arrogant woman who went about the house with a rod in her hand. Sometimes she flogged the houseman, sometimes the cook, and when she went to Mass and the other women did not give her place, would lay violent hands upon them. She stayed at Imola for a while, had many lovers and lived lewdly.' Yes, that about fits the Contessa."

"Oh dear! Doesn't sound at all the kind of person for you, Toby. Did you have a very bad time with her?"

His eyes twinkled at her. "Well, you do rather put me through the wringer on your behalf, you know. It's not an experience I'll forget in a hurry."

They sought out Father Antonio, who confessed to them that he had not told the Contessa of Lorenzo's death. "I couldn't do it," he said simply, "to take away her last hope, to lay that heavy burden upon her when she was so near death herself—no, I could not do it." He sighed heavily. "But I shall say my prayers for her poor, tormented soul."

"If you see Francesca Volci," Toby told him, "you can tell her that Alexander Dimola will see that she is recompensed for the money she gave his half brother."

Again the priest sighed. "Ah, yes! The money will be welcome, no doubt, but nothing can repay her for her other loss, can it? She sorrows, poor thing, because it was she who urged him on to go to America, to go to his death. Lorenzo, with all his faults, was a man who was terribly unlucky when it came to the women in his life."

"Indeed he was," Penny agreed, thinking of Inga.

They picked up the wine from the enthusiastic Enrico and were urged by him to return one day and visit the new "albergo" the village was planning. "At the rate things get done around here," Toby remarked, as they wound back down to the plain, "that should take twenty years at least."

They drove back at a leisurely pace through the burgeoning spring of France to the wet spring of England, arrived soggy but thankful in the venerable city of Oxford, and went directly to their equally venerable offices in the Pitt-Rivers Museum. Toby was deeply immersed in his own pile of mail when Penny burst into his office, waving a green slip of paper in her hand. "Look what I got from Alexander Dimola," she chirruped excitedly, and plonked it down under his nose. "My first fee, $5,000—isn't that terrific!"

"Are you going to keep it?" Toby demanded in a shocked tone. Never having had to give a thought to money himself, he tended to be very stuffy when it came to matters of business.

"I don't see why not. After all he did *ask* me to find Wanda's murderer, which I did. And it's not as if it'll make a dent in the Dimola fortune." She took up the check and waved it dreamily. "Just think, being *paid* to solve a crime, it opens up vast new vistas before my aging self."

"That's just what I'm afraid of," Toby said with deep gloom.

"I also got a long letter from him and one from Ann Langley as well," she continued happily. "They don't seem to hold the way things turned out against me—which is great, though I confess I'm a bit surprised."

"So, what has happened?" Toby tried to camouflage his curiosity but failed miserably.

"Well, they did charge Steven with manslaughter, but I'll be very surprised if he gets anything but a suspended sentence with Alexander in the fight. You know, maybe the demise of both their wives wasn't such a bad thing after all—now Alexander can marry somebody more suited to his station in life."

"What a horribly snobbish thing to say!" Toby was shocked.

"Snobbish but true. It struck me from the first that the Dimola women were decorative but lacked the clout—social and otherwise—that you'd expect in a family that well endowed. I'm sure Alexander will remedy that now he is mature."

"And how about Steven—do you think he and Ann Langley will get together?"

"I very much doubt it. I think that was a case of two raging romantics in an 'I-love-you-but-I-mustn't-touch' situation. Now they *can*, I don't think either of them will. Ann, I feel, has grown up a lot too, and has her eye firmly on Carson Grange. Her letter was Carson this and Carson that and nary a word of Steven. On Steven's part I think half of Ann's attraction lay in her resemblance to Annette—his first love, by all accounts. Steven's marriage to Inga had all the earmarks of a rebound affair. Also it obviously shook him when Ann so blatantly revealed that she thought *he* might have been the murderer. No, I wouldn't be a bit surprised that if dear old Dad doesn't come out of his operation, after a discreet amount of time Steven and Annette will make a match of it."

"Good God! Like a seventeenth-century Italian drama," Toby snorted. "Positively incestuous! And Rinaldo is going to risk the operation?"

"Yes. Of course he was vastly solaced by the news his son and heir was not the murderer, but he is going to wait until Steven is off the hook and then have it. I don't really think he cares to live any more in his condition, and who can blame him? Still, Maria has a lot of faith in this Dr. Lavin, and so do I, so he might bring it off. I asked him to look at Zeb before I left, and he did something and Zeb came right out of his coma, roaringly anxious to 'tell all!' " She giggled suddenly. "He always did have a lousy sense of timing."

"Regular Mrs. Fixit, aren't you?" Toby growled suspiciously. "Going back to hold his convalescent hand?"

She grinned at him. "No, thank you! I think Zeb and I have thankfully seen the last of one another."

"And how about the nephew?"

She grimaced. "Well, he's O.K. physically, but the state police did give him the boot. However, Alexander has offered him a very good job as security officer for Dimola Enterprises, and he's dithering between doing that or going back to school under his Vietnam G.I. benefits to become a teacher. I think he'd be a very good one, but I imagine, from the tone of Ann's letter, that he'll probably plump for the high pay of the Dimolas and wedding bells with her. Not a bad ending all round actually."

"So what do you plan to do with your loot?" demanded Toby.

A dreamy look came into Penny's face, and she perched herself on the edge of his desk. "Oh, I'm going to get a new car—a Triumph Spitfire, a bright green one like John's."

"What! One of those instruments of torture! You must be out of your mind. I can think of nothing more unsuitable for a woman of your age and position!"

"Oh, rubbish! It's a really zippy little car, just right for me. Why don't you like the idea?—want a cut of the loot?" she added crudely. "Come to think of it, you did have rather an expensive time of it."

"Certainly not! I have no desire to join the ranks of professional detectives." Toby was at his stuffy best. "But if you're flinging your money about, you could send a donation to Father Antonio on my behalf—God knows the poor man could certainly use it and he was a great help to me."

"Good idea! I'll do that." She jumped up and started to bustle out of the door, then stopped halfway out and turned. "All the same," she said defiantly, "I *am* going to get the Triumph—as Albert says, 'It's a nice little car.'" And closed the door with a decisive bang.

Toby looked at the closed panels of the door in exasperation. "And who the hell is *Albert?*" he demanded.